SPRING
STORM

BY TENNESSEE WILLIAMS

PLAYS

Baby Doll & Tiger Tail
Camino Real
Cat on a Hot Tin Roof
Clothes for a Summer Hotel
Dragon Country
The Glass Menagerie
A Lovely Sunday for Creve Coeur
Not About Nightingales
The Notebook of Trigorin
The Red Devil Battery Sign
Small Craft Warnings
Something Cloudy, Something Clear
Stopped Rocking and Other Screen Plays
A Streetcar Named Desire
Sweet Bird of Youth
THE THEATRE OF TENNESSEE WILLIAMS, VOLUME I
    Battle of Angels, A Streetcar Named Desire, The Glass Menagerie
THE THEATRE OF TENNESSEE WILLIAMS, VOLUME II
    The Eccentricities of a Nightingale, Summer and Smoke, The Rose Tattoo, Camino Real
THE THEATRE OF TENNESSEE WILLIAMS, VOLUME III
    Cat on a Hot Tin Roof, Orpheus Descending, Suddenly Last Summer
THE THEATRE OF TENNESSEE WILLIAMS, VOLUME IV
    Sweet Bird of Youth, Period of Adjustment, The Night of the Iguana
THE THEATRE OF TENNESSEE WILLIAMS, VOLUME V
    The Milk Train Doesn't Stop Here Anymore, Kingdom of Earth (The Seven Descents of Myrtle), Small Craft Warnings, The Two-Character Play
THE THEATRE OF TENNESSEE WILLIAMS, VOLUME VI
    27 Wagons Full of Cotton and Other Short Plays
THE THEATRE OF TENNESSEE WILLIAMS, VOLUME VII
    In the Bar of a Tokyo Hotel and Other Plays
THE THEATRE OF TENNESSEE WILLIAMS, VOLUME VIII
    Vieux Carré, A Lovely Sunday for Creve Coeur, Clothes for a Summer Hotel, The Red Devil Battery Sign
27 Wagons Full of Cotton and Other Plays
The Two-Character Play
Vieux Carré

POETRY

Androgyne, Mon Amour
In the Winter of Cities

PROSE

Collected Stories
Hard Candy and Other Stories
One Arm and Other Stories
The Roman Spring of Mrs. Stone
Where I Live: Selected Essays

TENNESSEE WILLIAMS

SPRING STORM

EDITED WITH AN INTRODUCTION BY
DAN ISAAC

A NEW DIRECTIONS BOOK

Spring Storm is published by arrangement with The University of the South, Sewanee, Tennessee.

Thanks are due to the Harry Ransom Humanities Research Center, The University of Texas at Austin, where the original typescript is housed.

Special thanks are due to Thomas Keith for his invaluable help in preparing the manuscript and for suggesting the cover art.

Manufactured in the United States of America
New Directions Books are printed on acid-free paper.
First published as New Directions Paperbook 883 in 1999
Published simultaneously in Canada by Penguin Books Canada Limited
Book Design by Sylvia Frezzolini Severance

Library of Congress Cataloging-in-Publication Data

Williams, Tennessee, 1911-1983
   Spring Storm / Tennessee Williams ; edited, with an introduction, by Dan Isaac.
      p.   cm.
   ISBN 0-8112-1422-2 (alk. paper)
1. City and town life--Mississippi--Delta (Region) Drama.
2. Young adults--Mississippi--Delta (Region) Drama. I. Isaac, Dan, 1930- . II. Title.
      PS3545.I5365S66   1999   99-34761
      812'.54--dc21
                                       CIP

New Directions books are published for James Laughlin
by New Directions Publishing Corporation,
80 Eighth Avenue, New York 10011

TABLE OF CONTENTS

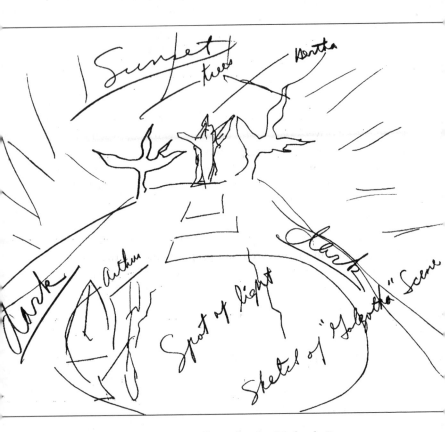

Sketch by Tennessee Williams for the "Golgotha" scene
at the end of Act One of *Spring Storm*.

INTRODUCTION

The first time I read *Spring Storm* was in the summer of 1984 during a two-week vacation, equally divided between visiting Anasazi sites in the Southwest, and an initial visit to the Harry Ransom Humanities Research Center (HRHRC) in Austin, Texas, to finally have a look at Williams' early unpublished full-length plays. When I came to *Spring Storm*, I read in a state of wonder. Having completed a doctoral dissertation for the University of Chicago in 1968 on Tennessee Williams' major plays, nothing in my research had prepared me for the power of *Spring Storm*. Clearly, this was the first work where Williams had staked out his world and found his life's calling.

When Williams began to write *Spring Storm*, he was twenty-six years old and still called himself Tom. Written and rewritten between 1937 and 1938, this full-length play depicting life and conflicted love in a small Mississippi Delta town during the Great Depression, is an unexpected treasure—something akin to an archaeological find. Furthermore, its remarkable quality is almost as surprising as its neglect and disappearance from the American cultural scene for more than sixty years. Hence this publication of *Spring Storm* is not simply a lost work recovered, but the addition of a fascinating and powerful work to the canon of America's greatest poet-dramatist.

In 1937 Williams had acquired a nice little reputation as a frequently published poet. In 1936, Harriet Monroe had written Williams that she would publish his poem "My Love Was Light" in her immensely prestigious *Poetry* magazine, the journal that had published modernist writers such as T.S. Eliot early on. So it should come as no surprise that the early working title for *Spring Storm* was "April is the Cruelest Month," the opening line of Eliot's most famous poem "The Waste Land."

The apparent mystery of non-production in its own time[1] is part of a larger saga that describes why and when Williams switched from writing short stories and poems, and decided to develop a new line writing plays. The momentous genre-change took place in Williams' life when a theater director named Willard Holland called him up in November of 1936, told him he had heard about his talent as a writer, and asked if he would take a shot at writing a "curtain-raiser" attacking military training on the campus of Washington University (in St. Louis) for a special Armistice Day theater program. Williams, who hated ROTC (and to his father's shame had flunked it at the University of Missouri in 1932) readily accepted Holland's challenge.

Willard Holland was a charismatic director who had turned a bunch of earnest amateur actors, members of a St. Louis theater company called the Mummers, into a spirited group ready to present socially engaged agit-prop plays in the best tradition of the Federal Theatre. Happily, Holland and Williams took to one another right away. Holland marveled at Williams' sparkling dialogue and ability to do fast rewrites; Williams delighted at finding a mentor who wanted his work.

When Williams told Holland of a play about a coal mine strike he had been trying to write, Holland encouraged him and held out the possibility of production. *Candles to the Sun*, a passionate protest play filled with grim heroes and the pathos of those who put their life on the line and sometimes lose it—with the cast singing "Solidarity Forever" for a curtain call—won the hearts of the audience, as well as the pen of the highly respected drama critic for the St. Louis *Post-Dispatch*, Colvin McPherson.

---

[1] *Spring Storm* was never produced in its own time, nor was it rediscovered at some later date when Williams was at the height of his career. *Spring Storm* would have to wait until the 1996 Octoberfest at Ensemble Studio Theatre in New York City where it had its first public presentation as a staged reading, which I initiated and organized.

And when this critic in his review of March 18, 1937, proclaimed the arrival of a new and eloquent theatrical voice, the career of a the future playwright, Tennessee Williams, had effectively begun.

A little more than a month after this triumphant opening, according to Willliams' diary note for April 25, 1937, he brought the first draft of his new play to Willard Holland:

> I have an appointment to see Holland at his study, 2:30
> . . . I'm delivering MS of my long play, "April is the
> Cruelest Month," but feel very uncertain about it.

Later, in two undated letters to Holland, left unfinished and unsent, Williams agonized over having brought the play to his newfound mentor, calling it "really a mess" in both letters. One can guess that Williams is responding to the embarrassment of Holland's disappointed response to a free-wheeling first draft. Holland did give Williams one piece of dramaturgic advice that Williams heeded. For in the second unsent letter, Williams begins in a state of exhilaration:

> I've just written a swell scene for the play. An outdoor
> scene like you suggested between Dick and Helen.[2] The
> only trouble is I'm afraid the rest of the play will be a
> hopeless anti-climax to this first scene, it is built up to
> such an emotional pitch.

Taking the play outdoors is truly the beginning of the transformation of "April Is the Cruelest Month" into *Spring Storm*, for not only the opening scene, but also the party scene in Act III ends with a cloudbursting thunderstorm.

On June 4th of the same year, a diary entry indicates that Williams had been making good progress with his "flophouse

---

[2] Helen is Heavenly's name in the earlier version of the play.

play," obviously a reference to the work that would be titled *Fugitive Kind* and produced by Holland in November of 1937 (not to be confused with *The Fugitive Kind*, the title of the film version of *Orpheus Descending*.) Unaccountably—for we know only what letters and occasional diary notes tell us—Williams seems to have abandoned *Spring Storm*.

*   *   *

As anyone who reads the ancient Greeks well knows, unforeseen variables can turn the straight smooth road to the future into a roundabout detour. The first of many shocks and setbacks to Tom Williams and his new career as a produced playwright can be traced to sometime in the middle of June 1937:

> Holland called and wants to see me. He's going to take a Paramount screen test in Hollywood.
> I don't wish him any bad luck—but if he should get in the movies—what chance would I have in producing a play next season.

This prospective defection must have felt like abandonment to Williams—as well as to the rest of the Mummers—and the anxieties generated by the possibility of Holland's permanent departure generated a *coup d'etat* a year later. Sometime during the summer of 1938, when Holland had again gone to Hollywood, this time acquiring an agent, the Mummers elected a new board and cut off his salary, accusing him of being autocratic and favoring particular actors. A compromise was crafted for Holland to remain for the coming season of 1938-39, but this would prove to be a terminal year for both director and company. Sometime in November of 1939, Holland, who had now taken up permanent residence in Hollywood, wrote to Williams requesting a copy of his prison play (*Not About Nightingales*), informing him that the Mummers had hired a new director. The entire operation folded shortly thereafter.

But what had happened to *Spring Storm*? On May 30, 1938—before the Mummers revolution—Williams made a brief diary note: "*Spring Storm* announced in St. Louis but Holland has not yet seen the script." Williams' sense of trepidation was well earned, for he had worked hard on *Spring Storm* during the latter part of his 1937-38 year in the theater department at the University of Iowa; but the response in several playwriting seminars was intensely negative. Two diary entries pretty much tell the story. The first is dated April 29, 1938:

> Badly deflated by Conkle and class this morning when they criticized my new play. Hardly a favorable comment. — Conkle hesitated when I asked him if it was "worth working on" — and said, "Well, if you've got nothing else" — Yes I was horribly shocked, felt like going off the deep end. Feared that I might lose my mind.
>
> I don't believe the play is that bad—its virtues are not apparent in a first reading—but I think it would blossom out on the stage.

Elsworth P. Conkle was a shy, self-effacing playwright-professor whose play about Lincoln, *Prologue to Glory*, had just been produced by the Federal Theatre (March 15, 1938) to critical acclaim. He and Williams had a good relationship and Willliams seemed to feel that Conkle was sympathetic to his work. Hence this cool rejection struck with particular force.

The final consideration of *Spring Storm* came during the summer session and Williams leaves a clear record of the response and his own personal despair.

> Aug. 2. (1938)—Read the final version of my second act and it was finally, quite, quite finally rejected by the class because of Heavenly's weakness as a character. Of course it is very frightening and discouraging to work on a thing and then have it fall flat. There is still a chance they may be

wrong—all of them—I have to cling to that chance. . . .
Holland is about my last resource. If he likes it and will
produce that would give me a spar to hang onto for a few
months. I would do better to come back here but how?
Mabie won't get me a scholarship.

The reference at the end is to Professor E.C. Mabie, the creator-head of Iowa's innovative theater department, who had also
been the ideological architect of the Federal Theatre, and who
remained a friend and advisor to its head, Hallie Flanagan, during this landmark theater's brief tumultuous life. Fervently promoting socially engaged theater, Mabie insisted that his students
write Living Newspapers, the investigative documentary genre
developed by the Federal Theatre in New York, first administered
by Elmer Rice. Dividing his class into pairs, he assigned Tom
Williams and Hayes Newby to write a Living Newspaper on
socialized medicine—which apparently has disappeared.[3]
Noted as a strict disciplinarian with a ferocious temper,
Mabie ran the theater department like a marine boot camp, training his students in every aspect of the theater, even turning his
playwrights into actors and prop managers. Feared as well as
revered, Mabie was called The Boss by students and colleagues
alike—and may well have been Williams' model for "Boss
Whalen," the sadistic prison warden in Not About Nightingales,
the play Williams began to write two months after the devastating rejection of Spring Storm.

*   *   *

Unfortunately, Mabie's response to Williams was intense and
visceral. According to Lyle Leverich in Tom: The Unknown
Tennessee Williams, Mabie referred to Williams as "that pansy,"
having discovered an aspect of Williams that Williams himself

---

[3] Lyle Leverich reported that Mabie so hated Williams' "Living Newspaper" that he tore it
up. But Hayes Newby, who was his co-writer, said he never heard that and believes he would
have, had it happened.

had yet to recognize. And this virulent homophobic attitude must have filtered down to the top sergeants who taught his classes. One can only wonder if the air was so poisoned that nothing Williams wrote could have possibly received a fair hearing.

Perhaps the students in Williams' playwriting workshop intuitively understood that with *Spring Storm* Tom Williams was secretly pretending. He was pretending to be a poet; he was pretending to be a rich boy; he was pretending to be a confused woman; and he was pretending to be a heterosexual filled with romantic longings. Consciously or unconsciously, Williams designed one part of *Spring Storm*, the role of Arthur Shannon, as a "Portrait of the Artist as a Young Heterosexual." Where, his fellow students must have wondered, was the social protest?

Whatever Holland's personal assessment of *Spring Storm* might have finally been, he seems not to have been interested in presenting it in the fall of 1938—which may have reflected his own precarious position with the new board of the Mummers. Or it may have simply indicated Holland's greater interest in Williams' new play *Not About Nightingales*.

Toward the end of that year, Williams performed the most important *rite de passage* of his life: in December of 1938, he left St. Louis for New Orleans. On the way, he stopped to visit his grandparents in Memphis, and sent some of his full-length plays —including *Spring Storm*—to the Group Theater in New York. Though Williams did receive a commendation and monetary award for his collection of one-act plays, *American Blues*, no known record survives of a response to *Spring Storm*.

The last we hear of *Spring Storm* in this early period is a letter from Williams in Hollywood to his mother. Though he had been dismissed as a writer by MGM, the studio still looked to him when seeking a script for a star. Excitedly, Williams wrote his mother about an opportunity in a letter dated August 24, 1943:

> During my lay-off I've been busier than usual as Goldwyn Studios phoned me. They need a vehicle for

Teresa Wright and wanted me to submit any suitable material. I thought of *Spring Storm*, and so I wired for it, and prepared a film story treatment which has kept me busy. I turned it in a couple of days ago. If sold outright it would mean a good deal of money, anywhere from five to twenty-five thousand, but I won't look for that till it happens. As a stage play, I think it was not very good, so I have nothing to lose.

The story editor liked what Williams gave him, but a producer upstairs nixed it. Obviously, a story where a young unmarried woman has sex with her boyfriend for a year and doesn't get pregnant would violate Hollywood's coded mythology for sex and consequences.

But the important note here is Williams' view of the worth of *Spring Storm* and his readiness to sell the rights to it. Williams had finally accepted the Iowa theater department's negative view of *Spring Storm*. They had persuaded him—at least for a time—not to trust his own voice nor believe in his own unique talent.

*   *   *

In later years, Tennessee Williams would mention *Spring Storm* only once. The occasion was a piece in the *New York Times*, "The Past, the Present, and the Perhaps," celebrating the opening of *Orpheus Descending*, scheduled for March 21, 1957. Because *Orpheus Descending* was a rewrite of his first professionally produced play, *Battle of Angels*, a legendary failure that closed on the road in Boston in January of 1941, a flood of memories from his apprenticeship years washed over him, and he served up a great memorable story about *Spring Storm*:

A third play called *Spring Storm* was written for the late Prof. E.C. Mabie's seminar in playwriting at the University of Iowa, and I read it aloud, appropriately in the spring. When I had finished reading the good professor's eyes had a glassy look as though he had drifted into a state of trance. There was a long and all but unendurable silence. Everyone seemed more or less embarrassed. At last the professor pushed back his chair, thus dismissing the seminar, and remarked casually and kindly, "Well, we all have to paint our nudes!" And this is the only reference that I can remember anyone making to the play. That is in the playwriting class, but I do remember that the late Lemuel Ayers, who was a graduate student at Iowa that year, read it and gave me sufficient praise for its dialogue and atmosphere to reverse my decision to give up the theater in favor of my other occupation of waiting on tables.

This is a marvelous piece of comic mythic memory covering over a great embarrassment. For Williams' 1938 diary entries, contemporary to the day, described a student response—not anything Williams wanted to hear—but a response nevertheless. Hence the diary contradicts at least one aspect of Williams' carefully constructed 1957 tale. Furthermore, the reference to Mabie as "the good professor" who remarked "kindly" is an insider-gag, a howler to anyone who knew Mabie and his attitude toward Tom Williams.

In August of 1938, Williams had written a letter to Mabie asking for a grant; and to convince him of his earnestness, Williams described how he had been hanging out at public beaches and a local flophouse so that he could pick up authentic local dialogue for the flophouse play. One can, alas, imagine Mabie reading the letter with a superior smirk, thinking to himself that this playwright-*poseur* was simply cruising. So this whimsical story of "How I Almost Gave Up Playwriting" is Williams' nasty-nice way of getting back at the man who once thwarted his desperate wish to be allowed to continue at Iowa on a grant in order to rewrite *Fugitive Kind*.

There is, though, one true note that stands hidden behind this 1957 tale. Not in the final draft of *Spring Storm*, but in a one-page alternative ending to "April is the Cruelest Month," there does indeed exist a shocking event that could justify the "paint our nudes" remark. At the top of this single page there is the following heading:

For the professional stage this ending might be substituted.

With Helen and Arthur alone on stage at night, we get the following:

HELEN: Listen—you can hear the rain fallin' out there . . .

> [*She sighs and makes a slight movement in the dark.
> The dress falls in a white cascade round her feet.*]

ARTHUR [*breathlessly*]: Helen!

> [*Long pause: then very softly and in a voice that
> contains all the sad, bewildering ecstasy of youth—*]

HELEN: Let's go out in the back-yard where you smelled those roses last night! [*Faint glimmer of lightning outlines her statue-like form.*]

CURTAIN

This alternative ending for "April Is the Cruelest Month" is sensual and dramatic—and presents great temptations from a theatrical point of view. But it is *not* the ending of the final version of *Spring Storm*, which is actually more subtle and surprising—though admittedly less provocative and sensational.

Regarding this final version: there seems to be but one surviving text and it is owned by the Harry Ransom Humanities Research Center (HRHRC) in Austin, Texas, and is a part of its Tennessee Williams Collection. On the cover of this *Spring Storm* text there is a handwritten note: "Return:— / Audrey Wood / #30 Rockefeller Plaza / New York City—"; and above the title there is a handwritten note: "For Play Contest." This contest might well have been one sponsored by the Theatre Guild to which he also submitted *Candles to the Sun*.

From Williams letter to his mother about MGM's interest in a vehicle for an actress, it is clear that Williams got a copy of *Spring Storm* by wiring his agent Audrey Wood. But at some point, he must have taken *Spring Storm* from her—taking it in effect out of circulation—and put it either in storage in New York, or sent it home to his mother, who would put it in her basement with all of Williams' other early manuscripts, for Edwina Dakin Williams presciently preserved anything in her possession that her writing son recorded on paper.

In 1962, Andreas Brown, bibliographer extraordinaire and now owner of the Gotham Book Mart in New York, asked Tennessee Williams for permission to rescue the old manuscript material stored in both his mother's basement and a New York storage locker. Permission was granted and Brown in 1962 deposited all these plays, versions of plays, letters, stories, poems, and diaries with the HRHRC, where they reside today. It was Brown's deposit that began their sizeable Tennessee Williams Collection. At the time Tennessee wrote to Andreas Brown from his home in Key West (10/1/62) that "I am longing to see this great mass of juvenilia you collected in Mother's warehouse, though I doubt it would have much interest to anyone but you and me." Apparently, he never did look at the material, and how very wrong he was about its interest to others!

Since the deposit of *Spring Storm* at the HRHRC in 1962, no biographer or academician has published a plot description of the play, let alone an adequate and responsible evaluation of it—with the single exception of a Japanese scholar, Akira Shida, who published an article "*Spring Storm* and *Not About Nightingales*: Two Unpublished Plays of Tennessee Williams"—and it was written in Japanese and never translated into English. After my presentation of the *Spring Storm* at the Ensemble Studio Theater in 1996, Allean Hale described the play in her essay, "Early Williams, the Making of a Playwright," included in *The Cambridge Companion to Tennessee Williams* (1997).

*   *   *

Spring Storm encompasses far more than the concerns of one couple—and Franz Wedekind's *Frühlings Erwachenen* (*Spring Awakening*, 1890) may have been an influence with regard to subject matter. Each character in *Spring Storm* is in his or her own way tied to the larger life, culture, and mores of Port Tyler—modeled closely on Clarksdale, Mississippi.

Clarksdale is the Delta town where Tom Williams spent his earliest and happiest years, living from time to time with his maternal grandparents. Because his grandfather, Walter Edwin Dakin, was the Episcopalian minister in Clarksdale, he knew everyone in town, and the Reverend loved sharing the local gossip with his alert grandchild who accompanied him when he made house calls.

Spring Storm takes place in 1937 over the course of four to eight days,[4] and it centers on four vibrant and articulate young people. Its plot is compact and focused; it is also nicely symmetrical, employing a Chekhovian strategy and structure where none of the four lovers has his or her love reciprocated. It is also Marxian insofar as each lover crosses over class lines for his or her love object.

Of the play's four protagonists, it is Heavenly Critchfield, rebellious and beautiful, who is at the epicenter, and much of the action swirls around her. The play's fluidity comes from her attempt to hold on to one man, Dick Miles, whom she desperately loves, while entertaining another, the strange and hapless would-be poet, Arthur Shannon, who has been obsessed with her since grade school. Heavenly is clearly in the middle when her mother discloses the family's economic difficulties, brought on by the Depression, and demands that Heavenly consider marriage to Arthur, son of the richest man in town.

Heavenly and Arthur share the stage by themselves for greater playing time than any other pair of *Spring Storm's* would-

---

[4] The number of days depends on the day of the week assigned to the church picnic. The problem of time in relation to sequential events will be discussed in the Textual Notes.

be lovers—a dramaturgic fact as curious and ironic as Tosca addressing her last words in the opera to Scarpia, challenging him to meet her again "before God." Heavenly and Arthur, in contrast to the other two, are simultaneously involved with someone else. And the two characters of lower-class origins, Hertha Neilson and Dick Miles, whose lives never intersect, stand on the outer rim of the action, each appearing in but two of the play's eight scenes.

In terms of literary archetypes, as well as for his own unique qualities, Richard Miles is a fascinating character. Rough-hewn and fiercely independent, apparently designed as a modern-day version of Huck Finn, who wants only to work on the levee to contain the swollen flood waters of the Mississippi or light out for South America, the new territory of choice, Dick's persona was perhaps also influenced by Eugene O'Neill's early vagabond years.

Hertha Neilson and Arthur Shannon are based mainly on projections of Williams' sister Rose and himself; while Heavenly Critchfield and Richard Miles are idealized types insofar as they are physically attractive, and both are driven by angry, rebellious temperaments.

One of the most affecting autobiographical moments in *Spring Storm* comes when Arthur gives Hertha his considered estimation of his own worth as a poet:

You see, my poetry, it isn't a terrific volcanic eruption—
No—it's just a little bonfire of dry leaves and dead branches.

When the poet, Tom Williams, matched himself against Ezra Pound and T.S. Eliot, he must have sadly but honestly realized that in his own writing of verse he was not an innovator. Still, Arthur Shannon's *mot juste* imagery here is very moving from a presumed minor poet. This character contains all of the playwright's weaknesses with few of his strengths. Had Williams not created Arthur Shannon, he might well have become him!

*   *   *

Spring Storm is a powerful play, and it might do well to list some of the play's qualities—and then to explain and account for them.

1. The plot in the second half of the play takes some unexpected turns, forcing a reconsideration of presumed certainties about how matters might be resolved.

2. The characters—as already briefly noted—are unique and memorable, based in part on firsthand experience.

3. One of Williams' trademark elements, the long lyrical aria, is employed repeatedly to reveal and enhance character, as well as to expound on symbols and idiosyncratic ideas.

4. An original and authentic time and place—a small town in the Mississippi Delta during the spring of 1937, toward the end of the Depression—help to delineate a poignant moment in American culture and history. In the Critchfield living room hangs the life-size portrait of Colonel Wayne, the family patron saint who led the charge up Cemetery Hill at Gettysburg, which brings the definitive, formative event of the past, the Civil War, physically and palpably on stage. References to a possible flood by means of the titular spring rainstorms recall a constant peril; while brief references to the continuing Depression, including the declining price of cotton, suggest that FDR's economic recovery programs never quite reached this corner of the South. Perhaps most important is the unforeseeable future: American involvement in a European war to defeat Hitler, called to mind only in hindsight by Dick's scornful attack on the daily routines of lower middle-class workers: "Pretty soon they'll be settlin' down in their overstuffed chairs to look at the evenin' papers. Gettin' the news of the day. . . . What happened in Czechoslovakia at eleven A.M." All of these factors contribute to the making of an epic play.

*   *   *

With regard to plot: throughout most of *Spring Storm,* Heavenly Critchfield commands both our attention and respect. In Act II, when her mother browbeats her for carrying on a year-long sexual relationship with her boyfriend, Dick Miles, our sympathies are strongly drawn to Heavenly. Esmeralda Critchfield—an officer in both the D.A.R. (Daughters of the American Revolution) and the D.O.C. (Daughters of the Confederacy)—commands her daughter to confess her sexual sins to the painting of Colonel Wayne that dominates the living room. Heavenly at first refuses, but as her mother continues to harangue, Heavenly finally approaches the portrait on the verge of tears—then unexpectedly blurts out: "Aw, go back to Gettysburg you big palooka!"

But in the last act something happens to this sympathy. Dick Miles, covered in mud, bursts into the Lamphrey's lawn party and asks Heavenly to marry him. But this proposal includes living on a river-barge near where he has begun to work, shoring up the levee against the rising flood waters of the Mississippi. Heavenly—anxious, torn, desperate—pleads with him: "I can't live like that! Don't ask me to!"

Dick gives Heavenly no options. Either his way or no way at all. When Dick starts to leave, she knows she is losing him and cries out: "Oh, Dick! Don't, don't! *Please don't!* The next day when Heavenly explains to her aunt why she rejected Dick's offer of marriage, her attitude has hardened and what she says startles and shocks:

> He wanted me to go with him. Me! Live like a nigger on
> a lousy barge!

Heavenly has begun to think and behave like her mother, and our response is to stiffen and step back. This angry use of the word "nigger" defines the social limits of her rebellion against the standards of her mother who has rejected Dick for not having the right kind of blood and background. At this point, *Spring Storm* becomes what it has been edging toward from the very first scene in Mrs. Critchfield's living room: a sociological study of caste and class among upper-class whites in the Mississippi Delta during the Depression.

Later in this scene Heavenly will further alienate her auditors with denigratory remarks about Hertha. Only her unexpected move at the very close permits a return of some sympathetic feeling for her.

The presence of the word "nigger" is disturbing—but it is meant to be. Only a few times does it occur dispassionately as the every day generic reference to a black man. But this kind of thoughtless usage is even worse; for it is the linguistic *modus operandi* for maintaining psychic distance from members of a caste that suffered from the stigma of slavery less than a century before.

Mrs. Critchfield uses the word once when enraged at her black maid, Ozzie, who drops and breaks a treasured piece of china, and calls Ozzie a "triflin' nigger." Worth noting, Mrs. Critchfield once refers contemptuously to Dick Miles as "that triflin' boy,"—a verbal device for transforming him into a "white nigger"—which is just the way Mrs. C. feels about him.

*   *   *

The many great arias that belong to *Spring Storm* can best be appreciated by reading them in dramatic context. Dick Miles delivers three, two of which are marvelous descriptions of life on the Mississippi; the last one is as good a piece of dramatic poetry as Williams ever wrote, truly a romantic hymn to the great fabled river.

These arias also embody important and significant thought, announcing the grand themes of *Spring Storm* that give the action heightened significance. And the motif that dominates and drives the play is the concept of the Front Porch Girl, which Heavenly introduces into a conversation with Arthur. Triggered by her embarrassment at not understanding some of the words Arthur uses—such as "metaphysical" and "atavistic"—Heavenly's first response is to turn her handkerchief into a hand puppet that speaks for her. But suddenly she forsakes charm and angrily expresses her great fear—which she argues is a basic fear of all southern womankind: the fear of spinsterhood: "All the boys go No'th or East to make a livin' unless they've got plantations. And that leaves a lot of girls siting out on the front porch waitin' fo' the afternoon mail. Sometimes it stops comin'. And they're still sittin' . . ." As this speech continues and builds, it becomes implicitly a plea for the liberation of southern women.

Heavenly's impressionistic sociology is based on what every pre-World War II southern woman knew: that she was allowed a very narrow time-span to find a mate, from about the ages of 17 to 21; and if she had a long time boyfriend who suddenly left her, she was tainted and became taboo. Such a woman then had two basic choices: she could, like Alma in *Summer and Smoke*, pick up strangers at the train station and live a life of social ostracism—Blanche DuBois is an example of this type *in extremis*; or she could metaphorically, if not literally, stay on the front porch and live a life of repression and respectability, forever resigned to a life without sex.

In *Spring Storm*, Williams presents us with a whole gallery of characters who have settled for spinsterhood: the first and most sympathetic is Aunt Lila, Heavenly's paternal aunt who lives in the Critchfield home with the family; Birdie Schlagman, the head librarian who counsels Hertha how to adapt to this kind of life; Hertha herself, who believes she has lost Arthur to Heavenly; and finally Agnes Peabody, who has become so much a living caricature of this type that she is laughed at behind her back. Within Williams' entire canon, this archetypal Front Porch Girl will never again be seen in such great profusion and sharp focus.

*　　*　　*

There are other arguments in *Spring Storm* worth noting, for they use "nature" as a referent.

One comes at almost the very end when Arthur kisses Heavenly, and she is surprised by her own response, and tells him that his kisses arouse the same sexual feelings in her as Dick Miles' kisses. So that true loss of innocence doesn't come with loss of virginity for Heavenly, but comes later with the discovery that she doesn't need Dick to pull the trigger of her desire, because desire is located in her body and not in the mystical in-between area of a relationship. Any man can do it for her, even the seemingly asexual Arthur. That surprising discovery is the real loss of innocence.

Significantly, Heavenly's discovery is related to *Spring Storm's* major dramatic flaw: Arthur forces himself on two different women; and in each instance, his persistence is arguably close to a sexual assault. In each case, the woman at first resists and complains, but as Arthur continues his relentless aggression, each woman melts and begs for more—all of which fulfills ancient male fantasies that every woman wants sex, but must be brought by force to this recognition.

The other argument from nature comes from Heavenly's deferential father, Oliver Critchfield, when they meet late at night in the living room (in the only scene added to the play from the outtake pile—see Textual Notes) and have their first hard drink together, a *rite de passage* of sorts; and Heavenly becomes very much the little girl with her Daddy, asking the most naive kind of question that is finally as profound as Job's quest for justice:

> Why can't people be happy together? Why can't they want the same things, instead of—fighting and torturing and—hating each other—even when they're in love?

And her father slowly responds:

> I guess those things are sort of natural phenomenon. Like these spring storms we've been having. They do lots of damage. Bust the levees, . . . destroy property, and even kill

people. What for? I don't know . . . I s'pose they're just
the natural necessary parts of the changing season. . . .

This answer points to ungovernable and inexplicable forces—a
confession that we can describe these chaotic forces but not
account for them, suggesting a world and universe with neither
design nor purpose.

Finally, in the thought department, *Spring Storm* contains the
first instance of Tennessee Williams' obsession with time.
Surprisingly, it comes from Heavenly at the Lamphrey's lawn
party, when she recalls a geology class field trip and tells Arthur
with a great deal of attendant sadness:

Just think one day we'll be fossils, too.... It won't matter
who we got married to or whether we lived to be old or
died young. They won't care; it won't make any difference to them. We'll just be marks on a piece of rock.

Here is the first evidence that Williams had discovered the
pathos of time. The great loss suggested by millions of years
became a personal imperative to Tom Williams: Remember!
Preserve! Describe! Record the life and times of the one happy
place of your childhood! Record it with such care that cultural
anthropologists will learn about mating habits and social gather-
ings! And how class standing was determined more on the basis
of family history and ownership of land, than personal liquidity
and money in the bank. But now at the very moment of this play,
these values were beginning to change.

And when people, ages and ages hence, want to know what
life was like in a small town in the Mississippi Delta during the
Great Depression of the twentieth century, go tell them: Find
Tennessee Williams' *Spring Storm* and read there!

Dan Isaac
New York
August, 1999

EDITOR'S ACKNOWLEDGEMENTS:

My gratitude to Joyce Fulton, Penny Mayfield, John Ruskey, all citizens of Clarksdale, Mississsippi, whose knowledge of local people and places has enriched the Textual Notes that accompany *Spring Storm*; and to Judy Flowers for her role in organizing the 1998 and 1999 Clarksdale Tennessee Williams festivals and inviting me to participate in them.

Appreciative thanks to Al Devlin and Nancy Tischler for sharing those TW letters that referred to SS, and for their expression of informed opinions about them, even as they were hard at work preparing a two-volume edition of TW's *Selected Letters* for publication by New Directions in the near future.

Special thanks to friends Aileen Baumgartner and Lee Zimskind for their critical reading of SS, as well as their insightful thoughts and feelings about the play.

And great thanks particularly to Peggy Fox, Vice President of New Directions, whose active engagement in the exploration of the *Spring Storm* text and its problems helped this writer appreciate the complexity of its problems.

My work on the editing of *Spring Storm* and the writing of its Introduction and Textual Notes is dedicated to my late wife Margaret Parker Isaac, a southern woman who would have certainly loved this play; and to our daughter Marina, who will someday come to love it.

—D.I.

SPRING
STORM

PLACE: Port Tyler, a small Mississippi town on the
Mississippi River

TIME: Spring, 1937

ACT ONE: A high bluff overlooking the Mississippi River on a
spring afternoon

ACT TWO:
Scene One: The Critchfield home, the afternoon of Friday,
the same week
Scene Two: Same, that evening
Scene Three: Same, three in the morning

ACT THREE:
Scene One: Lawn of the Lamphrey residence, the next evening
(Saturday), a party is in full swing
Scene Two: The Port Tyler Carnegie Public Library, the same
evening
Scene Three: The Critchfield home, late afternoon toward
evening of the next day (Sunday)

Spring Storm was first performed publicly as a staged reading in New York City on October 26th and 27th, 1996 as part of the Ensemble Studio Theatre's Octoberfest 96—Sixteenth Annual Festival of Member-Initiated Plays. Curt Dempster, Artistic Director; Jamie Richards, Executive Producer. The reading was directed by Dona D. Vaughn and initiated by Dan Isaac. The stage managers were Brian George and Sherry Stregack. The cast, in order of appearance, was as follows:

DICK MILES	Tristan Fitch
HEAVENLY CRITCHFIELD	Melinda Hamilton
REVEREND HOOKER	Dan Isaac*
AGNES PEABODY	Catherine Campbell
ETHEL ASBURY	Carolyn Marcell
SUSAN LAMPHREY	Ina Bass-Filip
MRS. LAMPHREY	Amy Coleman
ARTHUR SHANNON	Peter Sarsgaard
HERTHA NEILSON	Diana LaMar
LILA CRITCHFIELD	Celia Weston
ESMERALDA CRITCHFIELD	Dolores Sutton*
OLIVER CRITCHFIELD	Peter Maloney*
MRS. DOWD	Debbie Lee Jones*
MRS. BUFORD	Amy Coleman
MRS. ADAMS	Kristin Griffith*
HENRY ADAMS	Chris White
FANNY	Ina Bass-Filip
MRS. KRAMER	Debbie Lee Jones*
BIRDIE SCHLAGMANN	India Cooper
MABEL	Amy Coleman
RALPH	Brian George
STAGE DIRECTIONS	Mark Johannes

*denotes member of Ensemble Studio Theatre

This version of *Spring Storm* also includes the following characters which were not part of the version prepared for the Ensemble
Studio Theatre reading:

RONALD ASBURY
OZZIE
JACKSON

ACT ONE

SCENE ONE

The house lights go down. Children's voices are heard singing "Here We Go Round the Mulberry Bush," interspersed with laughter and shouting.

The curtain rises to reveal a high, windy bluff over the Mississippi River. It is called Lover's Leap. On its verge are two old trees whose leafless branches have been grotesquely twisted by the winds. At first the scene has a mellow quality, the sky flooded with deep amber light from the sunset. But as it progresses, it changes to one of stormy violence to form a dramatic contrast between Heavenly's scene and Hertha's. The atmospheric change is caused by the approach of the spring storm which breaks at the scene's culmination.

Dick is discovered alone on the bluff. He is a good-looking boy, say about twenty-three or four, tall and athletic in build, with a fund of restless energy and imagination which prevents him from fitting into the conventional social pattern. Out of ten such men, or maybe a hundred, one becomes an Abraham Lincoln or a Clarence Darrow, and the rest live out their lives in frustrated rebellion. Maybe Dick will be the chosen one or maybe he'll just be one of the ninety-nine: that will depend upon future accidents of life which his author will not pretend to foresee.

The singing continues from below, then fades out in scattered shouting.

Heavenly enters. The important thing about Heavenly is that she is physically attractive. She has the natural and yet highly-developed charm that is characteristic of girls of pure southern stock. She is frankly sensuous without being coarse, fiery-tempered and yet disarmingly sweet. Her nature is confusing to herself and to all who know her. She wears a white skirt and sweater with a bright-colored scarf.

HEAVENLY: Dick! What are you doing up here?

DICK: Watchin' the rivuh. She's risen plenty since mawnin'. See how she's pushed up Wild Hoss Crick up there no'th o' Sutters? Ole man Sutter's gonna go to bed some night in the state o' Mississippi and wake up in Arkansaw. That is, if he's lucky. If he isn't lucky he's gonna wake up a hell of a lot fu'ther south'n *any* state in the Union. Now if they'd just put that breakwater ha'f a mile fu'ther—

HEAVENLY [*exasperated*]: Dick!

DICK: Yeah?

HEAVENLY: Why do you walk off by yourself like this, honey? It looks peculiuh to people.

DICK: Does it?

HEAVENLY: Of cou'se it does!

DICK: I'm sorry. I stuck it out as long's I could. But those guessin' games got my goat—lissen to that! I used my five words in one sentence beginnin' with 'g' — guessin' games got my goat! No, that's just four.

HEAVENLY: That's remarkable, honey—you're a remarkable man, but I wish you'd pay some attention to what I'm sayin!

DICK: What're you sayin?

HEAVENLY: I'm sayin it looks peculiuh to people when you come up here by yourself and leave me down there.

DICK: Well, why don't you come up here, too?

HEAVENLY: Because I can't. It's impolite, Dick.

DICK: Aw, politeness! Bein' a damn hypocrite, that's politeness! —Me, I don't truck with politeness, I do like I please!

HEAVENLY: Dick, you're tryin' to aggravate me!

DICK [*laughing*]: Sure I'm tryin to aggravate you. Honey, I like to aggravate you.

HEAVENLY: I know you do. You take the greatest delight in getting me aggravated.

DICK: Sure I do. Cause when you get aggravated you're just as cute as a nine-tailed catawampus— Lookit that nigger down there in a flatboat tryin' to pull into shore. Bet he don't make it! Lookit by God! He's lost an oar!

HEAVENLY: Never mind that nigger. You come on down to the picnic.

DICK: Guessin' game over yet?

HEAVENLY: An hour ago.

DICK: I hope so. There's some things a grown man in his right senses can't put up with an' one of 'em's havin' some ole maid ask him what she's thinkin' of that's red, white, an' blue and begins with 'f'—I felt like sayin' "Your fanny!"

HEAVENLY: Dick!

DICK [*grinning slowly*]: She wouldn't have understood. She would have said, "No, suh! My name is Agnes!" —That's her now comin' up the hill with that balmy sky-rider.

7

HEAVENLY: Shh, Dick!—That's Miss Peabody an' Reverend Hooker!

[These two appear from below, a conventional, affable Episcopal clergyman and a coquettish spinster bubbling with animation.]

AGNES: I told her it was strongly reminiscent of something I'd seen in the *Atlantic Monthly*. Not that I'm accusing you of plagiarism, I said, but when there is such a startling similarity—

DR. HOOKER [*ignoring her prattle, heartily*]: Well, Richard, my boy, why aren't you down there participating in some of the big athletic events?

[*Everybody speaks simultaneously—confused chatter with a background of singing.*]

AGNES: Of course there was nothing I could do about it. Her parents were furious—

HEAVENLY: Hello, Dr. Hooker.

DR. HOOKER: How are you dear? If I remember correctly this young man of yours was quite a power on the high school football team back in—when did you graduate, Richard?

RICHARD: Thirty-two.

DR. HOOKER: Your laurels are still green, my lad, your laurels are still green—glorious sunset, Heavenly, glorious.

AGNES: Dr. Hooker, look at those clouds!

DR. HOOKER: And how does it happen your mother isn't with us this afternoon?

AGNES: Those clouds, Dr. Hooker.

HEAVENLY: Mother was very skeptical about the weather.

DR. HOOKER: Yes, storm clouds— "Swear not by the inconstant—April! Her moods are various—"

AGNES: Yes, but, Dr. Hooker—

HEAVENLY: I hope the picnic's a financial success.

AGNES: Yes but—

DR. HOOKER: Oh, indeed, yes. Richard, we're going to have the cake sale.

AGNES: Yes, but from the purely esthetic point of—

DICK [*indifferently*]: Yeah?

DR. HOOKER: Purely esthetic, yes!

AGNES: Such a beautiful cumulus formation in all my life!

DR. HOOKER: I presume you'll wish to make a bid for the young lady's culinary masterpiece! [*He laughs.*]

VOICE BELOW: Dr. Hooker!

AGNES: Oh, they're calling you Dr. Hooker!

DR. HOOKER: Coming! Coming!

AGNES [*following him off*]: It's the potato race, they're going to have the potato race! Wait for me, wait for Dr. Hookuh!

[*Exeunt. Dick has turned his back to the others and is still looking out from the bluff.*]

HEAVENLY [*slipping her arm through his*]: Still watching the river?

DICK: Sure. [*Dick turns around and moves back up to look at the river.*]

HEAVENLY: Can't I compete with the river?

DICK: Not right now.

HEAVENLY: Why not?

DICK: It's goin' somewhere.

HEAVENLY: Oh! So'm I. [*She starts off. He grabs her arm.*]

DICK: No, you're a woman. Women never go anywhere unless a man makes 'em. Don't you know what's the real diff'rence between the sexes?

HEAVENLY: Yes, I mean, no. I don't want to hear any dirty jokes.

DICK: This isn't dirty, this is scientific. Set down an' I'll tell you. The real diff'rence is that a man knows that legs're made to move on but a woman thinks they're just for wearin' silk stockin's.

HEAVENLY: You're crazy. I haven't got any stockings on mine.

DICK: Naw. But as Agnes would say they're "purely exthetic!" Ornamental—ain't that what she means?

HEAVENLY: Why shouldn't they be?

DICK: That's right. Why shouldn't they be?

HEAVENLY: You'd be the first to complain if they weren't.

DICK: Sure— But don't you get restless sometimes. Don't that river-wind ever slap you in the face 'an say, "Git movin', yuh damn l'il goober digger, git movin'!"?

HEAVENLY: No.

DICK: It does me.

HEAVENLY: You're gettin' one of your restless spells?

DICK: I'd like to follow that river down there—find out where she's goin'.

HEAVENLY: I know where it's goin' an' I'm not anxious to follow. Gulf of Mexico's the scummiest body of water I ever refused to put my feet in. Crawdads an' stingarees an'—

DICK: Aw, is 'at where it's goin? I thought it was goin' further'n that. I thought it was goin' way on out to th' Caribbean an' then some. I didn't think it would stop till it got clear round th' Straits o' Magellan!

HEAVENLY: What is this? A geography lesson?

DICK: Naw. It hasn't got a damn thing to do with geography.

HEAVENLY: Oh. You're speaking symbolically about the Gypsy in you or something. Every spring you get restless like this and talk about goin' off places.

DICK: Time I got started.

HEAVENLY: You mean it's time you stopped. It's gettin damned monotonous. —Even way back in grade school you had spells like this. Used to make me play hooky so we could watch the trains coming in.

[*Pause. The children are playing another singing game. Their voices float up with a melancholy sweetness.*]

DICK: That was fun, huh?

HEAVENLY: Not for me. I was terribly bored.

DICK: Then what did you tag along for?

HEAVENLY: Because I was crazy about you just like I am now. I was always secretly hoping that you'd get romantic and try to kiss me or something, but you never did. You were never interested in anything but trains, trains! I tried everything I could to distract you, even hid behind cotton bales to make you look for me, but it never did any good.

DICK: Was that why you kept hiding from me?

HEAVENLY: I'd been reading *The Sheik* —I wanted to be pursued an' captured an' made a slave to passion!

DICK: On a station platform?

HEAVENLY: Anywhere. I was very romantic in those days.

DICK: Sort of precocious for thirteen.

HEAVENLY: But you weren't a damn bit. It was two years before you finally kissed me.

DICK: An' then you didn't like it.

HEAVENLY: Not the first time. It was an awful anticlimax to what I'd expected. [*She kisses him; he suddenly draws her against him with real passion.*] —Mmmm. Your technique has improved a little since then. [*She wipes the lipstick off his mouth.*]

DICK: So's yours.

HEAVENLY: I couldn't have been so bad even then. I made you stop looking at trains.

DICK: Yes, you did that.

HEAVENLY: And now I've made you stop watchin' the rivuh—haven't I?

DICK: Not quite.

HEAVENLY: Liuh!

DICK: I still like to watch things goin' places.

HEAVENLY: My idea of goin' places is to make a success of things where you are.

DICK: Sure. Provided you're in the right place.

[*He rises and stretches. The singing has ended. An excited woman's voice —*]

MRS. ASBURY [*off-stage*]: Ronald! Oh, Ron-*ald*! [*She appears, a dumpy little matron in slacks.*] Oh Heavenly! Have you seen my child? Hertha Neilson's getting ready to tell the children one of her charming little fairy stories, and I don't want Ronald to miss it.

HEAVENLY: Sorry but I haven't seen him.

DICK: Is he a short fat kid with buck teeth wearin' glasses?

MRS. ASBURY [*outraged*]: Why, no!! —I mean—uh— [*She tries to laugh.*] That's not a very flattering description! Which way did he go?

DICK: Down that-away. Tow'd the Devil's Icebox.

MRS. ASBURY: The Devil's— ? Oh, Heavens! [*She goes off shrieking her son's name.*]

HEAVENLY: You should've offuhed to help her find him.

DICK: Hell. She needs to run some a' the lard off that carcass of hers.

HEAVENLY: Dick! —Dick, you know we've got to have some kind of social position when we get married, and we can't without bein' nice to people like Mrs. Asbury.

DICK: That's what I'm scahed of.

HEAVENLY: You mean you're scahed of marriage?

DICK: You remembuh that high-school play we acted in? Honey?

HEAVENLY: *Satuhday's Children?*

DICK: Yeah, there was one swell line in that play.

HEAVENLY: What's that?

DICK: Marriage is last year's love affair.

HEAVENLY: Oh! You don't want marriage!

14

DICK: Not the kind that ties ropes around people. [*He goes to the edge of the bluff.*] Listen to those whistles blowin'. They're gettin' out now. Pretty soon they'll be settlin' down in their over-stuffed chairs t' look at the evenin' papers. Gettin' the news of the day. Who went to Mrs. Smith's afternoon tea. What happened in Czechoslovakia at eleven A.M. Who's runnin' for gov'nor in the state of Arkansas. Ain't that somethin' for you, you bastards, you poor beer guzzlers. Tomorrow you'll wake up at half past six with alarm clocks janglin' like hell's own beautiful bells in your ears. The little woman will get her fat shanks out of bed an' put on the coffee to boil. At a quarter past seven you'll kiss her good-bye, you'll give her a cold eggy smack on the kisser. She'll tell you to remember your overshoes. Or to stop at the West End butcher's for a pound o' calves' liver. Don't forget, Papa. Papa, for God's sake don't forget to bring home that thirty cents worth of calves' liver. That's good, that's sweet of you, Papa. —Bye-bye! [*He turns slowly back to Heavenly.*] And they call that *livin'* down there. I got another word for it, Heavenly, and it don't commence with an "l"!

[*Mrs. Asbury's voice is heard calling Ronald. Dick continues, mocking.*]

"Ronald, oh, Ron-*ald*!"—don't fall an' break your fat little neck! —Christ, Heavenly, I want to get away from that sort of stuff down there. That's what I mean when I say I want to go places!

HEAVENLY: I know. You talk just as though I didn't exist.

DICK: Oh, I know you exist.

HEAVENLY: No you don't. You think I'm completely out of the picture. But I'm not. I think I'm pretty much involved in your plans for the future whether you know it or not.

DICK: I haven't got any plans for the future.

HEAVENLY: Yes, you have. I've got some for you.

DICK: Yeah?

HEAVENLY: I was talking to Dad last night. He says Mr. Kramer's willing to put you on at his office as soon as buying picks up.

DICK: Tell your Dad I'm much obliged but I don't want a job in Mr. Kramer's office or anybody else's. I don't want a white-collar job.

HEAVENLY: You prefer to work around a drugstore?

DICK: No, I prefer to get the hell out of here.

HEAVENLY: You want to go on the bum?

DICK: I want to do something worthwhile.

HEAVENLY: What is worthwhile in your opinion?

DICK: I don't know. Maybe if I did some traveling I'd find out.

HEAVENLY: All right. Let's take a round-the-world cruise.

DICK: I'd rather take a cattleboat to South America. [*He quickly rationalizes his impulse.*] There's lots of business opportunities down there. I could get into radio or engineering or—

HEAVENLY: Oh. Don't let me stop you!

DICK: Don't worry, it's just a pipe dream.

HEAVENLY: Worry? Not me! I guess you think I'd be sitting at home knitting socks till you came back with a long white beard to reward my patience. No, not me! "Faithful unto death" isn't the sort of thing I want carved on my tombstone.

[*Enter Susan Lamphrey, a fat girl of Heavenly's age.*]

SUSAN: Heavenly, you missed it!

HEAVENLY: Missed what?

SUSAN: The auction! Guess who bought your cake?

HEAVENLY: Who bought it?

SUSAN: Arthur Shannon. Paid eighty dollars for it.

HEAVENLY: You're foolin'!

SUSAN: I hope to fall dead if I am. I nearly did anow. And he came with that girl who works at the library. Hertha Neilson. I wonder how *she* felt? —Hello, Richard. Goodness, you are the exclusive Mr. Somebody! I didn't even know you'd come to the picnic! Oh, what I wanted to ask you—before I forget—I'm givin' a little lawn party in honor of Arthur Shannon this Saturday evenin' an' want you to come, Heavenly—an' bring along Dick!

HEAVENLY: Thanks. We'll come.

SUSAN: I've got to rush down there an' help pack things up. Bye-bye! [*She rushes off.*]

DICK: You can count me out.

HEAVENLY: Dick.

DICK: You know I don't mix with those kind of people.

HEAVENLY: All right. Don't put yourself out. I'll go with Arthur Shannon. He deserves some reward, anyway, for payin' eighty dollars for that little coconut cake! [*Dick turns his back.*] Saturday Arthuh will take me to the Lamphrey's lawn party.

DICK: Is he?

HEAVENLY: Yes. And Sunday evenin' we're going to the Country Club for supper. [*There is a tense pause.*] An' on the way home he'll ask me to marry him.

DICK: —Will he?

HEAVENLY: Yes! I know how to work those things.

DICK: Yes. You're very clever.

HEAVENLY [*bursting out*]: And you, you can take that river barge down to New Orleans an' ship out on a cattleboat if you want to. You can go clear down to the Straits of whatever-you-call-it 's far's I'm concerned! If you're restless, if you want to get rid of me so bad, don't think I'm gonna stand in your way! [*She turns away, sobbing convulsively.*]

DICK [*slowly*]: You know that's not true. You can't make me jealous about that little milk-fed millionaire's brat. Suckin' a sugar-tit all his life. I remember him in grade school before he went off to Europe. God, what a sissy! His chauffeur brought him to school an' called for him afterwards an' at recess he used to sit in a corner of the play yard readin' *The Wizard of Oz*. Remember how we used to serenade him when he drove up to school in his limousine?

> Artie, Smartie, went to a party!
> What did he go for? To play with his dolly!

HEAVENLY: Oh, you're disgusting!

DICK: You used to sing it yourself. I guess that's what gave him the nervous breakdown so he had to quit school an' be shipped abroad. He was kind of stuck on you even then, wasn't he? We used to kid you about the way he kept hangin' around you.

HEAVENLY: With Arthur's Shannon's prospects he can afford to have some faults.

DICK: Meaning I can't?

HEAVENLY: Exactly! Meaning just that. I've given up plenty of chances for you. In hopes you'd turn over a new leaf an' amount to something. Now I see that you never will. Arthur Shannon's going to ask me to marry him, and I'm going to do it.

DICK: You won't.

HEAVENLY: You just think I won't.

[He grabs her shoulders.]

Let go of me, damn you!

[She strikes him across the face. He draws back. They stand facing each other in the deepening dusk. —From below them comes the sound of the closing hymns at the church picnic—

> Now the day is over
> Night is drawing nigh,
> Shadows of the evening
> Steal across the sky.

The soft poignant quality of the hymn penetrates their mood and softens them both. Heavenly turns away, crying. Dick comes to her and embraces her gently. His voice is very low–]

DICK: Listen Heavenly! Honey, listen! You don't mean none of those things you just said. Why you couldn't shake me off anymore than you could your own skin. An' I couldn't either. —I've had my talk out. I'm always blowin' off my damn fool head about somethin'. But that's all over. Understan'? You and me, we'll get married this summer! Yeah. We'll have one a them June weddin's you see written up in sassiety columns with everything white an' sweet smellin' an' candles an' lilies an' yards an' yards of white lace for you to walk down like a queen with that new pipe organ playin' "I Love You Truly." An' me, I'll take that job of Mr. Kramer's!

HEAVENLY: Dick!

DICK: Sure . . . See those lights goin' on down there? One of them'll be ours! A little one off at the side—

[*He laughs gently. The closing hymn ends. There are sounds of general departure. Mrs. Lamphrey appears calling, "Ethel!"*]

MRS. LAMPHREY: Heavenly. Have you seen Mrs. Asbury? She's going home in our car.

HEAVENLY: She's gone after Ronald. He's exploring the Devil's Icebox.

MRS. LAMPHREY: Oh, that boy. Everybody's leaving; it looks so threatening!

HEAVENLY: Dick. Won't you hunt them up for Mrs. Lamphrey? I can't imagine what's keeping them so long.

MRS. LAMPHREY: Oh, I'd be so much obliged, Mr. Miles. [*She turns to Heavenly as Dick goes off.*] Richard is such a nice boy. I don't blame you, Heavenly.

20

HEAVENLY: For what?

MRS. LAMPHREY: For finding him irresistible. He has that—that sort of—primitive masculinity that's enough to make a girl lose her head!

HEAVENLY: Oh, I think I've kept mine.

MRS. LAMPHREY [*archly*]: Oh, do you? Good heavens, the storm's going to break any minute. And here comes Arthur Shannon with that Neilson girl. [*Calling.*] Arthur, did you ever see such a sky?

[*Arthur enters, followed by Hertha. He is a good-looking esthetic young man, about twenty-four. He wears white flannels, a sports coat, and a scarf about his throat. Hertha is thin and dark, about twenty-eight. Without money or social position, she has to depend upon a feverish animation and cleverness to make her place among people. She has an original mind with a distinct gift for creative work. She is probably the most sensitive and intelligent person in Port Tyler, Mississippi. Much of the dialogue following is simultaneous.*]

ARTHUR: Marvelous, isn't it? We're coming up to get a better view. [*To Heavenly.*] Hello!

MRS. LAMPHREY [*to Hertha*]: Oh, Miss Neilson, I enjoyed your little story so much. It was charming. Did you make it up yourself? Goodness! What wind! What wind!

MRS. LAMPHREY: Heavenly! Hadn't we better go down? This wind is terrific.

HEAVENLY: Oh, is that my cake Arthur? It was sweet of you to buy it.

HEAVENLY: I would have taken more pains if I thought it was going to bring such a big price. What is it Mrs. Lamphrey?

MRS. LAMPHREY: Don't you think we'd better go down?

ARTHUR: You won't forget about our dinner Sunday?

HEAVENLY : Oh, no. Yes, Mrs. Lamphrey! I'm coming.

MRS. LAMPHREY [*calling back to Hertha*]: Oh, Miss Neilson. Would you please remind your mother about those alterations to Susan's little pink blouse?

[*Hertha says nothing. Heavenly and Mrs. Lamphrey exeunt.*]

ARTHUR: Tired?

HERTHA: A little.

ARTHUR: It's your own fault. You would keep on climbing.

HERTHA: I wanted to reach the top.

ARTHUR: Well, now you're there.

HERTHA [*panting*]: Not quite. I'm going to save the rest till later. I'm going to wait till it's just the right color and then I'm going to go up the rest of the way—and then you'll probably hear me shouting "hello" to God!

ARTHUR: It *is* nice up here.

HERTHA: Lovely. I hate living on a flat surface. It's bad for you, Arthur.

ARTHUR: Is it?

HERTHA: Yes, you don't know how bad it is till you get up on a high place like this and see how your spirit expands.

ARTHUR: Is your spirit expanding?

HERTHA: Enormously, enormously! Don't you see how it's filling up the whole sky?

ARTHUR: Oh, is that your spirit?

HERTHA [*laughing*]: Yes!

ARTHUR: Congratulations! I haven't seen such a pyrotechnical display since July 14th, at Versailles!

[*Dick returns followed by the straggling Asburys.*]

RONALD: Aw, hell, Ma—

MRS. ASBURY: What did you say, Ronald?

RONALD: Nothing.

MRS. ASBURY: I'm afraid your father will be very angry when he hears about this. [*To Dick.*] Oh, Mr. Miles. I'm so grateful to you. —I hope you haven't lost Heavenly!

DICK: I reckon she's gone on with the others.

[*Exeunt all three.*]

HERTHA: We seem to be the sole survivors.

ARTHUR: Yes, thank heavens. I get so bored with those people.

HERTHA: Why do you bother with them?

ARTHUR: Have to. It's in the line of duty. I'm being groomed for the Planter's State Bank, so I have to make myself agreeable to depositors.

HERTHA [*seating herself on the hillside*]: Oh.

ARTHUR [*sitting beside her*]: Why do *you* bother with them?

HERTHA: I sort of—*belong* to them!

ARTHUR: How do you mean?

HERTHA: The Storybook Lady's a public institution.

ARTHUR: What?

HERTHA: The Storybook Lady—that's me! Every Tuesday, Thursday, and Saturday mornings, ten o'clock at the Carnegie Public Library. Have you ever heard what happened to the dark-haired princess in the magic tower when the handsome young prince went out to look for adventure? [*They both laugh.*] Oh, I don't mind that part of it. I like to make-believe as much as any of the kids. It's the old women that I can't stand, the ones like Mrs. Lamphrey who're so afraid that you'll forget your mother's a seamstress and your father's a night watchman at the lumber-yard who gets notoriously drunk every Saturday night! —Oh, they're very sweet to me, call me darling and send me flowers when I'm sick, but they take every precaution to see that I don't forget my social limitations— Did you hear Mrs. Lamphrey remind me about Susan's little pink blouse? Size forty-eight? — Know why she did that? She's worried you didn't know that mother took in sewing. She's worried about you and me—she thinks I'm trying to captivate you or something! [*She laughs.*] Of course things like that are only *amusing*, that's all!

[*Pause. Arthur lights a cigarette.*]

ARTHUR: You ought to get away from this place.

HERTHA: How could I?

ARTHUR: I don't know but there must be some way. You've got lots of talent and you're wasting it here.

HERTHA: So are you, wasting yours—at the Planter's State Bank.

ARTHUR [*lightly but with bitterness*]: No, I'm not wasting anything. In literature I'm one of those tragic "not quites"!

HERTHA: That's silly. You're terribly young still.

ARTHUR: I know my limitations. I haven't got it in me to be anything but a good amateur, I know that. You see, my poetry, it isn't a terrific volcanic eruption— No—it's just a little bonfire of dry leaves and dead branches. [*He laughs harshly.*] This morning I received an invitation to join the Junior Chamber of Commerce.

HERTHA [*pausing*] : Of course you refused?

ARTHUR: No. Accepted.

HERTHA: Arthur!

ARTHUR: Why not? Father was tickled pink—slapped me on the back three times and told me I was going places!

HERTHA: Did he tell you what places you were going?

ARTHUR: No. [*He laughs.*] There's no necessity for being explicit about such things—going places is just going places.

HERTHA: I see. [*Pause.*] Sometimes I wonder if anybody's ever gone anyplace—or do we always just go back to where we started? —I guess there's something significant about the fact that the world is round and all of the planets are round and all of them are going round and round the sun! [*She laughs.*] The whole damned universe seems to be laid out on a more or less elliptical plan. [*She rises.*] But I can't get used to it, Arthur. I can't adjust myself to it like you're doing— [*She gropes for words.*] —You see I can't get over the idea that it might be possible for somebody—sometime—somewhere— to follow a straight line upwards and get some place that nobody's ever been yet! [*Pause.*]

ARTHUR [*looking up at her with a slight smile*]: You mean to Paradise, don't you?

HERTHA: You're laughing at me. You think it's foolish.

ARTHUR [*slowly*]: I know what you mean. But I don't believe in it. I think it's just one of those romantic fallacies that everybody gets knocked out of him in the course of time. —Where are you going?

HERTHA: I'm going on up the rest of the way?

ARTHUR: To see God?

HERTHA: Yes. [*Arthur laughs.*] Don't you think I'll find him up there?

ARTHUR: Oh, you might! And then you *might* just find the other side of the hill!

HERTHA: Coming?

ARTHUR: No! I hate steep places. They make me feel like falling.

HERTHA: I love them. They make me feel like flying!

[*She climbs slowly up the hillside, Arthur remaining below. When she reaches the top, she stands there silently, silhouetted between the two dead trees. It has grown almost dark except for the magenta streaks of color in the fading sunset. The wind is beginning to rise, and there is a fitful glimmer of lightning.*]

ARTHUR: Well, have you found Him? [*Pause.*]

HERTHA: Yes!

ARTHUR: What does he have to say?

HERTHA: Oh, he doesn't say anything, he doesn't use any words—just a lot of beautiful gestures which I can't understand.

ARTHUR: What does he look like? The fatherly type?

HERTHA: No! —He's a very vague sort of person. He reminds me a little bit of an old Irishman who used to get drunk with my father on Saturday nights.

ARTHUR [*laughing*]: Yes?

HERTHA: An awfully funny old fellow— He never said much but he had a beautiful smile—especially when he was playing pinochle.

[*Arthur laughs.*]

You should come up and look at the river! It's marvelous! It's like a big yellow sea! [*Pause.*]

[*Arthur rises.*]

ARTHUR: That wind's too cold!

HERTHA: I like the taste of it.

ARTHUR: What does it taste like?

HERTHA: The outer edge of space. It's got the cold flavor of stars in it.

ARTHUR: That's the pine trees! You'd better come down and get into my trench coat, Miss Neilson.

HERTHA: I want to stay up here. I'm never coming down.

ARTHUR: Do I have to come up there and get you?

HERTHA: Yes, if you want me!

[*Arthur joins her above. The wind rises and blows Hertha's hair loose. They both point at things in the distance, talking and laughing, but the wind drowns their voices. Suddenly Hertha points upwards with a loud cry.*]

Wild geese!

[*If possible a faint honking should be heard as the geese pass over.*]

ARTHUR: Yes.

HERTHA: They're going up north to the lakes. —Why don't they take me with them?

ARTHUR: You're not a wild goose.

HERTHA: But I could be one—I could be anything that flies!

[*The wind roars about them.*]

ARTHUR: We'd better get down from here before we're blown down.

HERTHA: Not yet!

ARTHUR: Yes. Right now!

[*He jumps to the lower level, catches her waist and lifts her down with him. They descend to a lower level and seat themselves on the rocks. Arthur wraps his coat carefully about her. She looks at him silently—the wind falls.*]

HERTHA: Maybe the storm's blown over.

ARTHUR: No. This is just the traditional hush before it gets started.

HERTHA: If it storms lets stay up here! I love spring storms!

ARTHUR: If you caught your death of cold the kiddies would blame it on me—they'd say that I killed their Storybook Lady.

HERTHA: I'd like to die in a storm!

ARTHUR: Why would you?

HERTHA: I don't know. I think it's a good way of dying—Paul Cezanne died from painting in a storm.

ARTHUR: Did he?

HERTHA: Yes. I think that's the noblest death I ever heard of.

ARTHUR [*rising with a laugh*]: Hertha! You're getting morbid— we'd better go back down.

HERTHA: Give me a few more minutes!

ARTHUR: Gosh. [*She sits back down.*] You sound like Mme. Du Barry at the foot of the guillotine.

HERTHA: Did she say that? Poor thing. I know just how she felt— She had her head chopped off and tomorrow I'll be back at the Carnegie Public Library!

ARTHUR: You're terribly dissatisfied with things, aren't you?

HERTHA: Why wouldn't I be?

ARTHUR [*carefully*]: I wonder if it isn't because—

HERTHA: Because what?

ARTHUR: I knew a girl in London when I was going to school over there and she was terribly dissatisfied with things, too. We had a love affair.

HERTHA: Oh.

ARTHUR: It was her first experience and mine, too. It did us both good. We were both slightly crazy before it happened, and afterwards we were perfectly sane.

HERTHA: Why did you tell me that?

ARTHUR [*uncomfortably*]: I don't know exactly.

HERTHA: Did you think that my case corresponded to hers?

ARTHUR: No.

HERTHA: Did you suppose that fornication was the straight line upwards that I'd been trying to find?

ARTHUR: I didn't think I was putting it quite that crudely.

HERTHA: I'm sorry. You were trying to be very delicate about it.

ARTHUR: It just popped out.

HERTHA: I see

ARTHUR: We talk about things so frankly in Europe. I forgot that your southern puritanism might rise up in arms at anything too boldly stated.

HERTHA: I'm not offended. No I want to thank you for being so honest with me, Arthur. —How did this idyllic affair of yours turn out?

ARTHUR: The way you'd expect. We were both disappointed to find out that the world didn't burst into a million glittering stars simply because a man and a woman shared the same bed. But we got over that. She was very practical about it. She said it was in the interest of science or something, and the next summer she married a young M.P.

HERTHA: So now you're in mourning for her?

ARTHUR: No. Not for her.

HERTHA: For somebody else?

ARTHUR: Yes. A funny thing happened to me. I've just described one of those vicious circles that you were complaining about. I've come back to something that I went away from.

31

HERTHA: What's that?

ARTHUR: The girl in the white skirt.

HERTHA: Heavenly Critchfield?

ARTHUR: Yes.

HERTHA: What do you mean?

ARTHUR: I loved her a long time ago. When we were in grade school.

HERTHA: That long ago?

ARTHUR: Yes. It doesn't sound possible, but it's true. I was terribly shy and one day she laughed at me. After that I couldn't go back to school anymore. They had to send me to Europe.

HERTHA: Because she laughed at you?

ARTHUR: Yes. I thought I'd forgotten about it. But now I'm beginning to see she's been in me all the time, laughing at me—and everything that I've done since then has been a sort of desperate effort to— to—

HERTHA: To compensate for her laughing at you?

ARTHUR: Yes, that's it!

HERTHA: But now that you *do* understand it, you ought to be able to get away from it.

ARTHUR: That's the funny thing. I can't. I don't think I'll be able to get away from it until I've possessed her.

HERTHA: And made her stop laughing!

ARTHUR: Yes—yes, made her stop laughing.

HERTHA: And to do that you think you will have to possess her?

ARTHUR: Yes. Or somebody else!!

HERTHA: Somebody else.

ARTHUR: Who could make me stop thinking about her.

HERTHA: Do you think that anyone could?

ARTHUR: I don't know. . . .

HERTHA: Neither do I. . . . [*She rises.*] When did we start being serious?

ARTHUR: I don't know.

HERTHA: We shouldn't be. This isn't the serious season. It's the season for green things and frivolity and—

ARTHUR [*trying to catch her mood*]: And catching colds in the head.

HERTHA: Yes, the modern twist! The whimsical anticlimax! [*She jumps up to the second level.*]

ARTHUR: Where are you going?

HERTHA [*pointing gaily*]: You see those two old trees up there? I used to call them the two weird sisters—they look like they're putting a curse on the town!

[*The wind rises again with great force. There is lightning and a rumble of thunder.*]

ARTHUR: Hertha. Come down from there! It's starting to rain— the storm's breaking!

[*She waves to him gaily from the summit.*]

HERTHA: Look, Arthur! There's three of us now! We're putting a curse on the town. [*She laughs wildly.*]

[*Lightning outlines her figure between the two dead trees. There is a crescendo of wind and thunder—*]

CURTAIN

ACT TWO

SCENE ONE

The curtain rises on the living room of the Critchfield home. We leave the practical arrangement of this room to the scene designer with these suggestions:

It is furnished in good taste with the impediment of very limited funds and a passion for antiques that are not too well-preserved. Nevertheless the room has charm. It should have a pastel spring-like quality which should be accomplished by the use of light wallpaper with a floral pattern and a pleasing combination of pastel shades in the furnishings. Mrs. Critchfield is a foolish woman, but she has made a conscientious study of the women's fashion and home magazines.

There are a few essential features: a sofa with a table lamp on a table directly beside it; a large military-equestrian portrait of a Civil War hero hung prominently on the wall, preferably in a position that seems to command the whole room; a pair of French doors with white or cream curtains; a big chair with a floor lamp beside it; a bookcase or "secretary" and a radio cabinet.

As the scene opens, Aunt Lila is seated in her rocker close to the radio. It is important that this rocker should squeak audibly when in motion. Aunt Lila is a spinster with humor and charm. She shows evidence of having been beautiful in her youth and is by no means a conventional old maid. The doorbell sounds.

MESSENGER BOY [*offstage*]: Cutrere's.

MRS. CRITCHFIELD [*in the hall*]: Flowers? How lovely!

[*The door is closed. After a few moments, Mrs. Critchfield enters with a light blue vase of talisman roses which she sets down on the radio cabinet. Mrs. Critchfield is a woman with large hips, pearl eardrops, and pince-nez. Walking she always*

35

leans slightly forward from her hips like a kangaroo. Her mobile hands and quick jerky movements serve to emphasize this resemblance. She has a loud "cultured" voice and a manner that seems to be derived from a long career of presiding over women's clubs. On her breast are pinned emblems of the D.A.R. and D.O.C. She is always subconsciously aware of Colonel Wayne's presence in her domestic sphere and many times during the play we catch her glancing at his portrait as a source of continual moral support.]

MRS. CRITCHFIELD [*bustling into the room*]: A dozen roses from Cutrere's!

LILA: That Shannon boy send 'em?

MRS. CRITCHFIELD [*arranging*]: Of course!

LILA: What did you do with the old ones?

MRS. CRITCHFIELD: Threw them out.

LILA: When I was a girl I used to save the petals and make sachets.

MRS. CRITCHFIELD: Heavenly isn't quite that sentimental. [*She plumps down on the sofa with her sewing and a copy of* Vogue] Where is Heavenly?

LILA: Out.

MRS. CRITCHFIELD: I knew that much.

LILA: Well, that's all I can tell you.

MRS. CRITCHFIELD: Lila, what is that you're working on?

LILA: Some goods I got at Power's spring sale. It looked like a good buy so I bought it.

MRS. CRITCHFIELD: Your dividend come in from the compress stock?

LILA: It did.

MRS. CRITCHFIELD: My dear! Don't you think you might spend it a little more judiciously?

LILA: It's mine. I can spend it the way I want to.

MRS. CRITCHFIELD: Of course you can, my dear! But you might think of better ways than buying goods that will make you look like a holiday at the races.

LILA: This is for Heavenly to wear to Susan Lamphrey's lawn party.

MRS. CRITCHFIELD: Oh, now, that's sweet of you, Lila. But Heavenly's going to wear her white organdy.

LILA: What organdy?

MRS. CRITCHFIELD: Why, the one she wore at her high school commencement.

LILA: Land of Goshen. You can think of more ways to cheat the moths.

MRS. CRITCHFIELD: The material's perfectly good. I'm making it over by this new pattern in *Vogue*. [*She hands Lila the magazine.*] Princess sleeves with a little circular cape effect round the shoulders.

LILA: April's too early for organdy.

MRS. CRITCHFIELD: Not necessarily. —Everybody will be wearing summer formals.

LILA: Who said so?

MRS. CRITCHFIELD: Mrs. Lamphrey said so herself.

LILA: She just wants Heavenly to come looking peculiar so that fat Susan of hers won't show up so bad in comparison.

MRS. CRITCHFIELD: Now Lila. Why do you always attribute such awful motives to people?

LILA: Because I know 'em.

MRS. CRITCHFIELD: Know them nothing. You practically never go out of the house anymore. All you know is what Agnes Peabody tells you over the phone.

LILA: She tells me enough.

MRS. CRITCHFIELD: Yes, I'll have to admit she keeps well-informed.

LILA: Yes, speaking of information, she told me this morning that Mary Louise Shumaker's expecting another.

MRS. CRITCHFIELD: When?

LILA: Next October. I bet you Mary Louise hasn't found it out herself yet. —You'd think that Agnes was taking mail orders for the stork the way she scoops the town on things like that.

MRS. CRITCHFIELD: Lila, dear, can you see to thread this needle? I'm so nervous I can't hold it still. —Well, if I don't get finished I suppose she could wear her blue knitted suit.

LILA: That would be more sensible. April really is too early for organdy.

MRS. CRITCHFIELD: Everything's early this spring. [*She takes the needle.*] Thank you, dear. The crepe myrtle's been out a week.

LILA: What's that got to do with it?

MRS. CRITCHFIELD: I always start wearing white when the crepe myrtle's out. The boys are wearing white flannels. I saw Arthur Shannon in the public library this morning wearing white flannel pants and white shoes and a white sweater.

LILA: Trust him to do the outlandish!

MRS. CRITCHFIELD: I said to him, "My, my but you're all in white this morning!"

LILA: What did he say?

MRS. CRITCHFIELD: He said, "Yes, it's good cricket weather!" [*She bites off the end of the thread.*]

LILA: Cricket! What is cricket anyhow?

MRS. CRITCHFIELD: A game they play at Oxford. Terribly stylish.

LILA: Somehow I can't picture that boy playing anything more strenuous than checkers, and even then he'd probably have his chauffeur or valet or something to push 'em around for him.

MRS. CRITCHFIELD: Lila, dear, I want to ask you as a special favor to me to please desist from making those sarcastic remarks about Arthur Shannon and his parents, especially when Heavenly's around.

LILA: Why, I scarcely mention the Shannons! I haven't for twenty years! But why should I anyhow?

MRS. CRITCHFIELD: I'm hoping they'll make a match of it.

LILA: Heavenly and Arthur Shannon?

MRS. CRITCHFIELD: Yes. Do you have any objections.

LILA: —No. But I think Heavenly has.

MRS. CRITCHFIELD: Not if she's got any sense. Lila, you surely don't want her to make your mistake.

LILA: Which mistake do you mean?

MRS. CRITCHFIELD: Everybody expected you to make a brilliant marriage when you were a girl, but you spoiled all your chances by being a sentimental fool. You had a dozen good chances that you simply threw to the wind.

LILA: There was only one that I wanted.

MRS. CRITCHFIELD: You could have had *him*. You could have been sitting up there right now in the biggest house in town.

LILA: Yes, if I'd wanted to hold him against his will.

MRS. CRITCHFIELD: Let's not discuss that affair. It's one of those things that are better forgotten, especially when there's a young girl in the house.

40

LILA: You brought it up. I didn't. Don't think I'm turned against the boy on account of his father. If anything I'm holding *that* in his favor. I've still got lots of respect for Gale Shannon. The point I'm making is simply that Heavenly's been going with Richard Miles too long to switch to another.

MRS. CRITCHFIELD [*looking at her sharply*]: What do you mean?

LILA: Nothing but what I said.

MRS. CRITCHFIELD [*uneasily after a pause*]: I'm afraid there's been some gossip about Heavenly and that Miles boy. Mrs. Lamphrey said something right funny at the D.A.R. board meeting. She said she was glad that Susan hadn't centered her affections too definitely on any one boy, and she gave me the most pointed look, as if it had some special application to me or to Heavenly.

LILA: Centered her affections! That's good. The only thing that girl has ever centered is fat in the wrong places.

MRS. CRITCHFIELD: Lila!

LILA: Well, it's the truth.

MRS. CRITCHFIELD: It's painfully obvious that people are beginning to talk. And you can't altogether blame them. Heavenly is sometimes terribly indiscreet.

LILA: Is she?

MRS. CRITCHFIELD: You know that she is. And the Miles boy doesn't have a nice reputation. Didn't even get through high school and he's never been known to hold a job for more than two months at a time. One of these congenital loafers, that's what he is. Is that the kind of boy I want my daughter's name to be associated with? No, it is not!

LILA: I'm not saying that I approve of Dick Miles either. But love is something it's a mistake to interfere with.

MRS. CRITCHFIELD: Love! —If I were a girl I'd be thrilled by Arthur's attentions. He's got looks, money, social position—everything!

LILA: Except a backbone.

MRS. CRITCHFIELD: You're prejudiced against him, you're holding a grudge.

LILA: I'm holding no grudge. Arthur bores the girl to death sitting here reading poetry to her and talking about—

MRS. CRITCHFIELD: Is there anything wrong with having intellectual interests?

LILA: Not if they're reasonably unobtrusive. Oh, he's nice enough I suppose. But I wouldn't put too much stock in him as a prospective son-in-law.

MRS. CRITCHFIELD: Didn't he pay eighty dollars for Heavenly's cake at that church affair?

LILA: He doesn't know eighty dollars from eighty cents. Agnes Peabody says he's taken a notion to that librarian, Hertha What's-her-name, that went to the picnic with him.

MRS. CRITCHFIELD: Hertha Neilson? That girl's peculiar!

LILA: Is she?

MRS. CRITCHFIELD: Yes! She paints very odd pictures. —Wears her hair in braids like a schoolgirl and she's easily twenty-eight or thirty.

LILA: Anything else wrong with her?

MRS. CRITCHFIELD: Indeed there is. Her father's a drunkard and her mother takes in sewing. —You can imagine the Shannons allowing their son to get himself mixed up with that kind of trash.

LILA: Well, they're both artistic and Heavenly isn't.

MRS. CRITCHFIELD: Heavenly is quite artistic. Those teacups she painted in the eighth grade. Absolutely remarkable! What's happened to them?

LILA: Don't you remember? You gave them to Ozzie.

MRS. CRITCHFIELD: I didn't. —She must have acquired them in her usual way. —Arthur is just being nice to the Neilson girl because of her pitiful circumstances.

[The phone rings. Mrs. Critchfield rushes into the hall and can be heard answering phone in her flute-like company voice.]

Mr. Critchfield's residence— No. Heavenly is not in at the moment. Who's calling, please? Oh! [Her tone becomes icy.] No, she's out and I hardly believe she'll be in the rest of the evening. [She hangs up with a bang and re-enters living room.]

LILA: Richard Miles?

MRS. CRITCHFIELD: Yes. —Disgusting!

LILA: You shouldn't have cut him off so short!

MRS. CRITCHFIELD: Why shouldn't I? I'm sick and tired of that boy monopolizing Heavenly's time. [*She speaks from the window.*] There she comes up the walk now without any hat on and the rain just pouring. [*She crosses to the hall.*] I guess she thinks we haven't got worries enough without—Heavenly!

[*Mrs. Critchfield exits. Lila turns on the radio.*]

ANNOUNCER'S VOICE: —And for his first selection, your old friend and neighbor would like to read you a little poem by Sara Teasdale which seems especially appropriate to a rainy spring afternoon—

[*A recitation with organ background follows.*]

> When I am dead and over me bright April
> Shakes out her rain-drenched hair
> Though you should lean above me broken-hearted
> I shall not care
>
> I shall have peace as leafy trees are peaceful
> When rain bends down the bough
> And I shall be more silent and cold-hearted
> Than you are now!

[*Mrs. Critchfield re-enters near the close of the poem.*]

MRS. CRITCHFIELD [*referring to some act of Heavenly's*]: Insolence! What is that sob-stuff you're listening to?

LILA: The Village Rhymester.

MRS. CRITCHFIELD: Please use the earphones! [*She switches off the radio.*] Sentimentality is something that turns my stomach.

[*Aunt Lila quietly adjusts earphones and turns the radio back on. During the dialogue between Heavenly and Mrs. Critchfield, Aunt Lila is seen dissolving into tears as she listens to this, her favorite program—she dabs her eyes and her nostrils and looks dreamily at the ceiling—she finally blows her nose—it is evident that the Village Rhymester is giving his audience a thorough workout. Heavenly enters immediately after Mrs. Critchfield's speech directly above. Mrs. Critchfield continues.*]

What do you mean by running upstairs when I ask you a question?

HEAVENLY: Did you want me to stand there dripping rain all over the carpet?

MRS. CRITCHFIELD: Where have you been—the drugstore?

HEAVENLY: Yes.

MRS. CRITCHFIELD: What for?

HEAVENLY: A Coke.

MRS. CRITCHFIELD: We've got bottled Cokes in the basement.

HEAVENLY: I like fountain Cokes, Mother.

MRS. CRITCHFIELD: What was that package you were trying to hide in your slicker?

HEAVENLY: I wasn't hiding it, I was trying to keep it dry.

MRS. CRITCHFIELD: What was it?

HEAVENLY: Perfume.

MRS. CRITCHFIELD: Perfume!

HEAVENLY: One ounce of *Quelques Fleurs*. I didn't have a drop left.

MRS. CRITCHFIELD: Did you charge it?

HEAVENLY: Of course I charged it, mother.

MRS. CRITCHFIELD: Well, I suppose I shall have to have that account discontinued.

HEAVENLY: Suit yourself about that.

MRS. CRITCHFIELD: You don't seem to realize the financial condition this family's in.

HEAVENLY: Don't I?

MRS. CRITCHFIELD: No. For a girl of your age you show remarkably little sense about our account at Mungers. When I was twenty-two, I was married and keeping house. And believe me, I learned the value of every cent.

HEAVENLY: Yes, Mother. —Did anyone call?

MRS. CRITCHFIELD: Arthur called.

HEAVENLY: Who else?

[*Mrs. Critchfield says nothing.*]

I was expecting a call from Dick.

MRS. CRITCHFIELD: Didn't you see him at the drugstore?

HEAVENLY: No. He was out.

MRS. CRITCHFIELD: Imagine! A delivery boy.

HEAVENLY: He's not a delivery boy. He's assistant pharmacist.

MRS. CRITCHFIELD: Soda jerker.

LILA: Dick has never jerked a soda in his life. Besides, it's only a temporary job—Mr. Kramer's promised him something.

MRS. CRITCHFIELD: Did your father do that?

HEAVENLY: Yes.

MRS. CRITCHFIELD: Your father will just get himself in bad with Mr. Kramer. That Miles boy will never be able to hold a job.

HEAVENLY: He's going to hold this one.

MRS. CRITCHFIELD: You have a dinner engagement with Arthur, you know.

HEAVENLY: Yes, I know. Sunday night.

MRS. CRITCHFIELD: I think you should wear your blue knitted suit. It's really more stylish than ever. [*Heavenly rises.*] Where are you going?

HEAVENLY: I'm going to phone Dick.

MRS. CRITCHFIELD: Listen, Heavenly—

HEAVENLY: What?

MRS. CRITCHFIELD: If you let a chance like this slip through your fingers—

HEAVENLY: What chance are you talking about?

MRS. CRITCHEFIELD: Arthur Shannon.

HEAVENLY [*smiling wryly*]: Oh. [*She starts to leave.*]

MRS. CRITCHFIELD: Heavenly, come back here. I want to talk to you—you can call that boy later.

AUNT LILA [*huskily as she removes earphones*]: "—But only God can make a tree!" [*She rises and dabs her eyes.*] Shall I make tea for anyone else? Heavenly? Esmeralda?

HEAVENLY: No, thanks, Aunty.

MRS. CRITCHFIELD: No.

[*Lila goes out, still under emotional spell of the Village Rhymester.*]

MRS. CRITCHFIELD [*after a short, uncomfortable pause*]: How have you been feeling, dear?

HEAVENLY: Perfectly well, Mother.

MRS. CRITCHFIELD: I believe you've fallen off some.

HEAVENLY: Is that what you wanted to talk about?

MRS. CRITCHFIELD: No, it is not. When you assume that defensive attitude toward your mother, it makes it very difficult for her to discuss things with you. [*Heavenly lights a cigarette.*] You're smoking too much, Heavenly. It makes you nervous and cross and discolors your teeth. —Now what I wanted to say is—

HEAVENLY: Arthur Shannon?

MRS. CRITCHFIELD: Yes.

HEAVENLY: Please don't. [*She rises abruptly and crosses to the French window.*]

[*During this following speech, Mrs. Critchfield should acquire a certain dignity and force. She is talking about something she feels keenly which is the very core of her existence.*]

MRS. CRITCHFIELD: Don't you think that having the finest blood in America imposes on you some obligations? I'm sure that you do. It's a question of self-respect. But it's also a question of something deeper than that. Maybe I'm being old-fashioned. Hanging on to something that's lost it's meaning. I know that some people say so. But they're people who never had anything worth hanging onto. You're not one of them, Heavenly. A girl whose name is listed under five or six different headings in Zella Armstrong's *Notable Families* and every other good southern genealogy couldn't help but feel it her sacred duty to live up to the best that's in her. The Waynes, the Critchfields, the Tylers, the Hallidays, and the Brookes. You've got them in you, Heavenly. You can't get them out. And they're going to fight you to the last wall if you try to mix their blood with ditchwater!

HEAVENLY [*turning furiously*]: What do you mean?

MRS. CRITCHFIELD [*breathing heavily*]: I mean that Arthur Shannon comes from your kind of people and the other one doesn't. You're not going to throw him over for a boy whose people are so low, so common that—!

HEAVENLY [*screaming*]: Stop it! I won't listen to it!

MRS. CRITCHFIELD: You sit right back down there, young lady, and wait till I'm finished! There are certain practical considerations that I don't like to mention. You know what they are. The

Shannons are the wealthiest family in the Delta. They own fifteen thousand acres of land and Gale Shannon's President of the Planter's State Bank. I know that sounds cheap and crude and mercenary, and I could hardly force myself to say it. But I had to. You forced me to, Heavenly. —Your father's health is uncertain. I was talking to Dr. Gray about his last examination and it seems it was not as favorable as it might have been.

HEAVENLY: Nobody pays any attention to Dr. Gray.

MRS. CRITCHFIELD: No? He brought us into the world. He's been our family physician for nearly sixty years.

HEAVENLY: He's in his dotage.

MRS. CRITCHFIELD: Very well, just ignore my warnings. —Some day you'll have a sad awakening, young lady.

HEAVENLY: Oh, mother, I know, I know!

MRS. CRITCHFIELD: You *don't* know. But under the circumstances I think it best you *should*.

HEAVENLY: Know what?

MRS. CRITCHFIELD: Dr. Gray intimated that your father does not have much longer to live.

[*A pause: Heavenly is slightly stunned.*]

HEAVENLY: I don't believe it.

MRS. CRITCHFIELD: I've kept this from you all. I've borne it alone— Your father's hypertensive condition has been aggravated by business worries. It's taken a serious turn. And if something should happen on top of everything else—

HEAVENLY: You mean if Dick and I should get married?

MRS. CRITCHFIELD: Yes! Precisely! Would you be willing to sign your father's death warrant? And mine, too? Do you know that we haven't managed to put by a single dollar since the stock crash, and now with this business recession— Our account's been cut off at Mungers— It's not at all unlikely that we'll have to go on relief next winter.

HEAVENLY [*in a quiet strained voice*]: If you want me to marry Arthur Shannon, you might as well know right now that it isn't possible.

MRS. CRITCHFIELD: What do you mean?

HEAVENLY: I mean it isn't possible. [*She averts her face.*]

[*A pause while this penetrates Mrs. Critchfield's shocked brain.*]

MRS. CRITCHFIELD [*gasping*]: Heavenly! [*Then she speaks slowly.*] Has there been—? Have you—?

HEAVENLY: Yes. I *have*. That's the answer.

[*A strangling sound comes from Mrs. Critchfield's throat. Her suffering is too acute to be ludicrous—she looks desperately about the room, her antiques, her heirlooms, even Colonel Wayne's portrait, fail to support her in this moment. Heavenly lights a cigarette.*]

MRS. CRITCHFIELD [*choked*]: You dare to come into this house, in my presence and make that shameful confession?!

HEAVENLY [*with some of Colonel Wayne's courage*]: You asked for it and I'm not ashamed. We love each other. God knows that's not as immoral as what you want me to do! And I'm not going to do it.

MRS. CRITCHFIELD: I—I feel sick. —No, it isn't the truth, you've made this up, it's a lie!

HEAVENLY: It's not a lie, mother.

MRS. CRITCHFIELD [*because she can't face it.*]: It's got to be! Don't you understand? It's got to be— [*She sinks weakly on the sofa and looks at Colonel Wayne's portrait.*] You're never going to see him again.

HEAVENLY: Didn't you hear what I told you? We already belong to each other.

MRS. CRITCHFIELD: No. Not one more word! Or I'll report the whole thing to your father, even if it kills him. —So it *is* true. But I suppose it isn't too late?!

HEAVENLY: What do you mean?

MRS. CRITCHFIELD [*anxiously*]: Nothing's happened! You haven't gotten yourself in trouble, have you?!

HEAVENLY [*turning away in distaste*]: No.

MRS. CRITCHFIELD: Then it *isn't* too late. It can still be covered up.

HEAVENLY: Covered up?

MRS. CRITCHFIELD: Yes. You can leave town for awhile. Visit Aunt Clara down in Biloxi, in a month or two you'll—

HEAVENLY: I'm not going to give Dick up.

MRS. CRITCHFIELD: You've got to.

HEAVENLY: I can't. I'm not going to be an old maid.

MRS. CRITCHFIELD: You don't have to be an old maid.

HEAVENLY: Oh. You think Arthur Shannon would be willing to take me secondhand?

MRS. CRITCHFIELD: Does Arthur know?

HEAVENLY: I'd tell him.

MRS. CRITCHFIELD: No, you couldn't. You wouldn't have to. There's precious few girls that get married nowadays without having had one or two love affairs in the past.

HEAVENLY: Maybe not. But I've got a sense of decency.

MRS. CRITCHFIELD: *You* talk about *decency*!

HEAVENLY: Yes, I do.

MRS. CRITCHFIELD: You don't know what the word means.

HEAVENLY: It's you that don't know what it means. It's you that wants to make a prostitute of me.

MRS. CRITCHFIELD: Shut up! You dare to stand in front of me and say things like that. I don't know why I should let you kill me, you mean, despicable girl!

HEAVENLY: I haven't done anything terribly wrong. Dick and I loved each other—so much that—whatever happened it really wasn't our fault.

MRS. CRITCHFIELD: How long has it been going on?

HEAVENLY: For a year. Ever since last spring. I couldn't help it. I don't know how to explain. He lost his job at the planing mill and he was going to leave town—he was feeling so discouraged and restless and all—I couldn't bear it—I couldn't give him up—

MRS. CRITCHFIELD: And so to hold him you—

HEAVENLY: Yes. To hold him.

MRS. CRITCHFIELD: Without any shame you come to me and say that?

HEAVENLY: Yes. Without any shame.

MRS. CRITCHFIELD: You horrible, shameless, ungrateful girl!

HEAVENLY: Yes. [*She turns to leave.*]

MRS. CRITCHFIELD: Heavenly! [*Then with real feeling.*] Oh, my poor, poor daughter! [*She breaks down sobbing.*]

HEAVENLY [*slightly moved*]: I'm sorry mother. [*Pause.*]

MRS. CRITCHFIELD [*sobbing*]: When you were a little girl and did something wrong— I used to make you come in here and apologize to Colonel Wayne's portrait—don't you remember, Heavenly?

HEAVENLY: Yes.

MRS. CRITCHFIELD: That was because I wanted you to understand the responsibility of having fine blood in you. Heavenly—I want you to do that now. I want you to stand here in front of your great-grandfather's picture and beg his forgiveness for the first disgrace that's ever come to his name.

HEAVENLY [*stiffening*]: I won't do it.

MRS. CRITCHFIELD: You've got to. Your family's all you've got left, you poor girl. If you don't respect that you've got nothing. —You come here and tell Colonel Wayne you're sorry for those awful things you talked about in his presence—*Heavenly*!

HEAVENLY [*dully*]: Yes. [*She walks stiffly up to the portrait, stands before it, sobbing—then suddenly blurts out.*] Aw, go back to Gettysburg you big palooka!

[*She runs out of the room sobbing.*]

CURTAIN

Dinner has just been concluded. Mr. Critchfield slouches into the living room, thoughtfully manipulating a toothpick. He removes his coat and shoes and loosens his tie; he flops wearily into the big chair under the floor lamp and unfolds his evening paper to the market reports. As Lila enters, he mechanically extends a section of the paper to her with a muffled grunt.

LILA: No thanks, Oliver. I misplaced my glasses. [*She settles into her usual place by radio and picks up her sewing.*] How's cotton?

OLIVER: Off two points on the Memphis curb. One at New Orleans.

LILA [*glancing at him*]: Well, did you go to the clinic today?

OLIVER: Huh? —Yes. I went.

LILA: What did they tell you?

OLIVER [*sheepishly*]: Nothing wrong with my heart. Just gas on the stomach.

LILA [*relieved*]: I knew it! I get palpitations myself when I eat too many starchy things. Nervous stomach's the curse of the Critchfields. Alf struggled against it for years, so did Cousin Rachel.

[*From the dining room across the hall Mrs. Critchfield's strident voice is heard directing the colored servant.*]

MRS. CRITCHFIELD: Hurry up, get this table cleared off. I want the place to look decent in case Mr. Shannon comes in. No, no, you've been in the house twenty years and you still don't know where the percolator sits! No, take the dishes, take the dishes, I'll take care of the silver! Ozzie, be careful. Don't try to carry three things off at once, here, you let me—

[*There is a startled outcry from Ozzie and a crash of broken china. Mrs. Critchfield screams in agony.*]

MRS. CRITCHFIELD: Oh, my good— O*oooh*!

LILA [*with fatalistic calm*]: She broke another piece of Havilland.

MRS. CRITCHFIELD: Get out of here, you trifling nigger, get on back to the kitchen.

OZZIE: Yes'm, Mizz Critchfield.

LILA [*calling*]: What happened in there?

MRS. CRITCHFIELD: She broke another piece of the Havilland.

LILA [*sotto voce*]: It's no wonder. The way she devils that girl would drive a saint to distraction. [*She rubs her forearms.*] It's chilly, I've got goose pimples— [*She takes a few more stitches.*] Somebody must be walking over my grave . . .

[*Mrs. Critchfield charges into the front room. She stands stage center, her eyes shooting Olympian bolts at her husband's oblivious figure. She suddenly swoops down on him like a predatory hawk and snatches the newspaper from his hands.*]

MRS. CRITCHFIELD: Yes, to you it's a matter of complete indifference!

OLIVER: What the Sam Hill—!

MRS. CRITCHFIELD: No, Oliver, I shouldn't annoy you! I should go right on bearing the whole intolerable burden just as I've done the past twenty-three or four years.

LILA: Why don't you let him digest his dinner?

MRS. CRITCHFIELD: There are some things more important than digestion.

LILA: That's a matter of opinion.

MRS. CRITCHFIELD: You probably wouldn't think so. But I'm not willing nor able to bury my head in the sand like an ostrich when my daughter's whole future is at stake!

OLIVER: What's the matter with Heavenly?

MRS. CRITCHFIELD: It's high time you asked that question. Oliver, I've deliberately shouldered the whole thing myself because of your disinclination to accept any responsibility and also because of your health—

LILA: Stop carping on Oliver's health. —He's gone through the Memphis clinic this morning, and there's not a thing wrong with him except nervous stomach.

MRS. CRITCHFIELD: Oh! Well. Is this true?

[*Oliver clears his throat uneasily.*]

You didn't mention it to me? You didn't think it was necessary to relieve my mind of all the anxiety I've had to suffer because of your constant complaints?

LILA: I guess he wanted to break it to you gently. [*She switches on the radio.*]

MRS. CRITCHFIELD: But from what Dr. Gray said—

LILA: Dr. Gray said nothing. He never says anything except, "How's your bowels!"

MRS. CRITCHFIELD: Please! Will you turn that radio off? —There's something I've got to discuss seriously with Oliver, something that— [*Her voice breaks.*]

LILA [*rising*]: Mind if I take the comics? [*She winks at him and crosses offstage.*]

MRS. CRITCHFIELD [*with extreme acidity as Lila closes the door*]: It is sometimes difficult to believe that your sister comes of a genteel family. I suppose Heavenly's lack of principles is not entirely her fault.

OLIVER: If you mean she's a Critchfield, Ezzie, that's nothing to her discredit. —Whatever the girl has done or hasn't, I'm pretty sure it can't be as serious as your hysteria would make a person suppose.

MRS. CRITCHFIELD: Oh, no, it's nothing serious when a girl is being talked about by the whole town!

OLIVER [*a little anxious*]: Talked about, eh? I should consider it much more serious if she wasn't being talked about. [*There is a pause while he goes about filling his pipe.*]

MRS. CRITCHFIELD: Leave that pipe alone and listen to what I'm saying! —You've adopted that humorous tone too often in dealing with your child's problems. —This time it won't do.

59

OLIVER: All right, Esmeralda! When you've told me the cause of Heavenly's disgrace I'll be in a much better position to adopt a suitable tone of voice. What's she done this time?

MRS. CRITCHFIELD: For quite a while I've heard rumors—little insinuations—about Heavenly and that trifling boy she's been going with.

OLIVER: Richard Miles?

MRS. CRITCHFIELD: Yes! I chose to ignore it because I thought my daughter was above such things. Well, now I've discovered that I was mistaken.

OLIVER: Discovered what?

MRS. CRITCHFIELD: This afternoon right here in this room she came to me with the horrible, disgusting confession that— Oh. I don't know how I've managed to keep my senses.

OLIVER [alarmed]: What in tarnation are you driving at? What confession? Esmeralda!

[The sound of a car stopping is heard.]

MRS. CRITCHFIELD [in a sudden flurry]: Get those things out of here, those papers, your coat, your shoes! It's Arthur Shannon! — We'll finish this talk upstairs!

OLIVER: Good Lord!

[He belches and rubs his stomach. He crosses the room. Mrs. Critchfield hastily snatches up various articles, arranges sofa pillows and changes the position of her antique chair. She switches on the little museum light over Colonel Wayne's portrait and *then rushes out. Arthur enters first. His manner is markedly different from the first scene. His continental poise is lost, and he is awkward as an adolescent. He goes to the radio on which the roses are placed. Heavenly enters.*]

HEAVENLY [*removing her hat*]:   Lord, I'm glad to get this off! Arthur, I have a marvelous idea for a new spring hat. I'm going to pin a couple of roses on Aunt Lila's purple silk parasol. [*She crosses to Arthur.*] Oh, aren't they lovely! How did you know that talisman roses are my favorite flowers?

ARTHUR: Are they? I thought all girls preferred orchids.

HEAVENLY: I hate orchids.

ARTHUR: Hate them! Why?

HEAVENLY: Oh, I've seen 'em at debuts in Memphis and the girls that wear 'em are always those money-snobs who give you a look that peels the gilt off your slippers and puts ten years on your formal.

ARTHUR: Possibly if you wore one yourself you might overcome that aversion.

HEAVENLY: Yes. Possibly. Orchids are seen around here about as often as Haley's Comet. Gosh, me with an orchid! I wouldn't know what to do with it! I'd probably go parading up and down Front Street, holding it over my head and singing "The Star-spangled Banner"! [*She seats herself on the sofa.*]

ARTHUR: Or you might wear it to the Lamphrey's tomorrow night.

HEAVENLY [*springing up breathlessly*]:   Ahthuh!

ARTHUR: It was just an impulse. They weren't available at Mr. Cutrere's so I ordered one from Memphis.

HEAVENLY: You dahling! [*She hugs him.*] I'm—I'm completely flabbergasted! I'm so excited I could bust!

ARTHUR: I guess I should've surprised you with it, but when you said you hated orchids I was afraid you might be really allergic to them or something and so I—

HEAVENLY: Oh, no—no! I *love* orchids, I'm *crazy* about them! Gosh, me with an orchid! From Memphis? Won't that create a sensation! Oh, I can just see it in the society column— "Miss Heavenly Critchfield lived up to her name last night in a divine white creation with a regal orchid pinned to her shoulder!"

ARTHUR: What's a "divine white creation"?

HEAVENLY: Oh, that's my white organdy— Mrs. Dowd, the society reporter, thinks it's divine because it's so damned everlasting. I graduated in it about five years ago, and it's been getting more divine ever since till now it's about fit to be worn as a nightshirt by Jesus! Wait a minute, will you? [*She flies out of the room and is heard on the stairs—*] Mothuh! Aunt Lila! What do you think?

[*The upstairs door slams on her exuberant voice. Arthur goes hastily to the mantle mirror where he adjusts his tie and combs his hair; in a moment, Heavenly re-enters with two Coke bottles.*]

Mothuh was just tickled silly and so was Aunt Lila. I thought maybe I could get a new pahty dress to go with it but nothing doing. I've got to wear God's nightie. You'll have a Coke with me, won't you? [*She exits through the rear door.*]

ARTHUR: A what?

HEAVENLY [*from offstage*]: A Coca-Cola. Don't you know? It's a new kind of drink.

ARTHUR: No, thank you.

HEAVENLY [*re-entering*]: Why not?

ARTHUR: I never touch stimulants after six-thirty, especially when I'm not sleeping well.

HEAVENLY [*drinking rapidly from the bottle*]: Haven't you been sleeping well?

ARTHUR: No. Not lately.

HEAVENLY: Oh, that's a shame. [*She returns to sofa, finishes one bottle and starts on the second.*] What shall we talk about?

ARTHUR [*uncomfortably*]: Well, I—don't know!

HEAVENLY [*giggling*]: You know what mother said to me before we went out? She said, "Heavenly, you must try to choose intelligent subjects of conversation so that Arthuh won't get bored!" What do you think of that, Arthur? [*She takes another long gulp.*]

ARTHUR: I think it was quite unnecessary.

HEAVENLY: Yes. So do I. Because I really don't know any intelligent subjects of conversation. [*She laughs.*] I asked Mothuh what she meant and she said, "Oh, books and things!" I said, "Well, I know what books are but what's things?" And that made her furious, she turned as red as a lobster, and Aunt Lila and I both nearly died laughing— She called me an ignoramus! Which is perfectly true . . .

ARTHUR: I don't think it is.

63

HEAVENLY: Ah! That's terribly chivalrous of you. [*She finishes the second bottle, then leans back on the sofa.*] I feel like music tonight. Music and dancing. I hope we'll have fun at the Lamphrey's, don't you?

ARTHUR: Yes.

[*There is a constrained pause.*]

HEAVENLY: What are you thinking about?

ARTHUR: Pardon?

HEAVENLY: I said what are you thinking about.

ARTHUR [*very uncomfortable*]: Oh—things.

HEAVENLY [*with a slightly derisive smile*]: Books and things?

ARTHUR: No.

HEAVENLY: Just books?

ARTHUR: No.

HEAVENLY: Oh! Just *things*. That's nice. I wish I could think about things.

ARTHUR: Can't you? [*Heavenly shakes her head.*] Why not? [*Heavenly shrugs.*]

HEAVENLY: It's a wasted effort. It's a lot easier just to feel things and it's a lot more fun.

ARTHUR: Feeling some things isn't fun.

HEAVENLY: No, of cou'se not. But thinking about them doesn't help them any.

ARTHUR: Seems to me we're getting a little metaphysical here.

HEAVENLY [*wide-eyed*]: What's that?

ARTHUR: Metaphysical?

HEAVENLY: Yes.

ARTHUR: It's sort of— dealing with insubstantial matters.

HEAVENLY: Oh. Like books and things. [*She laughs.*]

ARTHUR: I always have a rather uncomfortable feeling when you laugh that way.

HEAVENLY: Why?

ARTHUR: I suppose you'd call it a sort of—atavistic emotion

HEAVENLY: A what?

ARTHUR [*confused*]: Nothing.

HEAVENLY: Oh—nothing. [*She smiles almost mockingly and lowers her eyes.*] Look. It's a bunny-rabbit. [*She has twisted her white handkerchief into the semblance of a long-eared rabbit's head.*] It's wiggling its ears at you. It says "Shame on Ahthuh fo' usin' such long words!" [*She laughs.*] It says, "If I went to school at Oxfo'd I'd be sma't too an' use big words, but I'm just a dumb little bunny that doesn't know anything but how to wiggle its ears an' eat grass!" [*Slowly, dreamily she shakes the handkerchief out—she smiles sadly and shakes her head.*] Poor bunny! He's all disappeared—he's just a little white hankie now. But he still smells nice. [*She lifts it delicately to her nostrils, glancing provocatively at Arthur from under her dark lashes.*] He smells like dead rose leaves. Mmmm. Aunt Lila makes your talisman roses into sachets when they're withered an' puts 'em in our handkerchief boxes— gives 'em such a sad, sweet smell. [*She smiles.*] Like old maids' memories, that's what it reminds me of! [*She sniffs the cloth delicately once more, and then smooths it thoughtfully on her lap. Suddenly she raises her face to Arthur's with a look of startling intensity.*] I'd rather die than be an old maid! [*Pause for emphasis.*]

ARTHUR: Surely that's not a possibility!

HEAVENLY [*intensely*]: Oh, yes it is. All the boys go No'th or East to make a livin' unless they've got plantations. And that leaves a lot of girls sitting out on the front porch waitin' fo' the afte'noon mail. Sometimes it stops comin'. And they're still sitting out there on the swing in their best white dresses, smilin' so hard it's a wonder they don't crack their faces—so people across the street won't know what's happened! "Isn't it marvelous weather? The sky's so perfectly blue! Mother and I put up six quarts of blackberry jam last night!" —*Oh, God!*— [*She rises quickly and walks over to the French window.*] That's why girls like me act so silly, Ahthuh, like music an' dancing instead of books and things, because we're scared inside, so scared it makes us feel sick at the stomach—

ARTHUR: Scared of what?

HEAVENLY: Of sitting out there forever on the front porch in our best dresses!

ARTHUR: That's quite understandable in the case of some girls.

HEAVENLY: But not in mine?

ARTHUR: Certainly not.

HEAVENLY: Thanks. But you don't know.

ARTHUR: Know what?

HEAVENLY: I made a mistake.

ARTHUR: In what way?

HEAVENLY: I—I loved the wrong boy.

ARTHUR: Oh. —You still do?

HEAVENLY: Yes. And now—

ARTHUR: Now?

HEAVENLY [*desperate fear showing in her face*]: Now he's trying to break away—he wants to work on the river! He'd like to get rid of me now!

ARTHUR: Has he said so?

HEAVENLY: No, but I can feel it coming. [*She smiles bitterly.*] Oh, my! [*She turns to the window, parts the curtains, and looks out with her back to Arthur. He looks at her, troubled, confused, his hands clenched.*] —I don't know why I should bother you with all this! [*She laughs.*] It's not your affair! [*She turns slowly back to him.*] It's starting to rain again—it makes such a sleepy sound I can hardly keep my eyes open. . . . [*She has returned to the sofa, draws her feet under her, and leans back provocatively. She looks at Arthur from under her lashes with a very slight smile.*] I hope that Mothuh doesn't come in. I'm not in what you would call a very ladylike position. However I'm too comfortable to care. [*She allows one arm to slip languidly from the sofa, fingers trailing the floor.*]

ARTHUR [*clears his throat and rises*]: Heavenly, I—

HEAVENLY: What?

[*He has started toward her and then, as if frightened, draws back. He mechanically removes a small book from his pocket.*]

ARTHUR: I wanted to give you this.

HEAVENLY: What is it?

ARTHUR: A book of modern verse.

HEAVENLY [*in a tone of final despair*]: Oh.

ARTHUR: It's an autographed first edition of Humphrey Hardcastle.

HEAVENLY: Oh.

ARTHUR: There's just a short passage I marked last night.

HEAVENLY: Oh.

ARTHUR [*fumbling in an agony of embarrassment. through the pages*]: Here it is.

HEAVENLY [*sadly*]: Please commence the reading.

ARTHUR: It's called "Apostrophe to a Dead Lover!"

HEAVENLY: It sounds so't of spooky.

[*Arthur springs up violently and flings the book to the floor.*]

HEAVENLY: What's the matter?

ARTHUR [*choked*]: Nothing! I don't know. I'm in a state of confusion! [*He crosses the room a few steps.*] I guess you think I'm a pretty queer sort of person. I am. I was brought up in a school for problem children, I've never had any normal relations with people. I want what I'm afraid of and I'm afraid of what I want so that I'm like a storm inside that can't break loose! Do you see?

HEAVENLY: No. not quite. [*She smiles at his back.*]

ARTHUR [*sharply*]: Why are you laughing at me?

HEAVENLY: I wasn't.

ARTHUR: You were — I could see you in the mirror!

HEAVENLY: I was only smiling a little.

ARTHUR: You smile like that a great deal. You used to smile that way when I knew you in grade school.

HEAVENLY: Can you remember me that long ago?

ARTHUR: Yes. Very clearly. Especially the way that you smiled.

HEAVENLY: I didn't know my smile was that hard to forget.

ARTHUR: Ordinarily it might not be. But I was sensitive.

HEAVENLY: You mean you thought I was making fun of you?

ARTHUR: I knew that you were.

HEAVENLY: I don't remember.

ARTHUR: Don't you remember that afternoon when a bunch of them cornered me in the recess yard and kept yelling "sissy" at me until I cried? You stood there laughing at me. I never forgot that afternoon. That was something I never got over. It wasn't the boys yelling sissy that hurt me so much. It was you—you standing there laughing at me the way you were laughing a minute ago when I caught your face in the mirror. That laugh, that was why I couldn't go back to school anymore—so they had to send me to Europe and say that I'd had a nervous breakdown.

HEAVENLY: You mean that was all on my account?

ARTHUR: Yes. On account of you.

HEAVENLY: Then I should think you would hate me.

ARTHUR: I did. I hated you.

HEAVENLY: You still do? Now?

ARTHUR: Yes. You don't get over things like that. When I saw you again this spring for the first time in thirteen years it was exactly the same. It started all over again.

HEAVENLY: You mean that afternoon at your mother's reception?

ARTHUR: Yes. When I came downstairs and saw you standing in the hall looking up at me with that politely contemptuous smile of yours—it was the same exactly—all you needed was a white hair ribbon and a handful of jacks!

HEAVENLY: You turned and went back upstairs.

ARTHUR: You must've been awfully amused.

HEAVENLY: I was. At Mothuh's disappointment.

ARTHUR: The next morning I called Cutrere's. Had them send you a dozen roses without any name.

HEAVENLY: What did you do that for?

ARTHUR: I don't know. Everything that I've done since then has been done by compulsion. If you only knew the heroic effort it took for me to ask you to the country club that first time.

HEAVENLY: Your voice sounded funny over the phone.

ARTHUR: I had butterflies in my throat. At lunch I kept dropping the silver.

HEAVENLY: I thought you were sick.

ARTHUR: I was.

HEAVENLY: But if I made you so miserable why did you want to be with me?

ARTHUR: You don't know much about psychology.

HEAVENLY: No.

ARTHUR: The reason I hated you was that I loved you.

HEAVENLY: *Loved* me?

ARTHUR: Yes.

HEAVENLY: I don't see how that's possible. You couldn't love anybody that you hated.

ARTHUR: Oh, yes, you could. Very easily. Strindberg says "It's called love-hatred and it hails from the pit!"

HEAVENLY: I don't know anything about Strindberg, but it doesn't sound practical to me. How could you be in love at that age?

ARTHUR: Thirteen's old enough. Of course, there wasn't anything consciously sexual about it.

HEAVENLY: I should hope not.

ARTHUR: I think you can love more at that age than any time afterwards. At least it's the hardest to get over.

HEAVENLY: But you *have* gotten over it *now*?

ARTHUR: Of course I haven't.

HEAVENLY: You mean you still—?

ARTHUR: Yes. More than ever.

HEAVENLY [*crossing to the sofa*]: I don't believe you. What you want is to have your revenge. Once you got me you wouldn't want me anymore. You'd leave me cold.

ARTHUR: No!

HEAVENLY: Yes, that's it. Whether you know it or not that's how it would be. No. Thanks! I'd rather take a chance on Dick. At least he's honest. It's none of your psychological business—we're really in love!

ARTHUR: Heavenly— [*He moves uncertainly toward her.*]

HEAVENLY: You'd better go now. I've got another engagement.

ARTHUR: Who with? Richard Miles?

HEAVENLY: Yes.

ARTHUR [*with childish cruelty*]: I've heard about you and him.

HEAVENLY [*stiffening*]: Have you?

ARTHUR: Yes. People have told me.

HEAVENLY: Who's told you what? That long-nosed mother of yours?

ARTHUR: You don't have to insult my mother.

HEAVENLY: I don't like having people gossip about my business.

ARTHUR: My mother's never mentioned your name.

HEAVENLY: Oh, hasn't she? I've heard different.

ARTHUR: You've heard that she gossips about you?

HEAVENLY: Yes. [*Her voice breaks.*] They all do.

ARTHUR: If he was the right kind he wouldn't expose you to that sort of thing. He'd respect you too much.

HEAVENLY: He didn't seduce me if that's what you mean. He didn't have to. I wanted him as much as he wanted me.

ARTHUR [*pausing*]: We're being childish, both of us. Deliberately hurting each other. It doesn't matter about you and that boy. I've had an affair myself with a girl in London.

HEAVENLY: One of those intellectual affairs?

ARTHUR: No. Quite the opposite.

HEAVENLY: That's sort of hard to imagine.

ARTHUR: Why is it hard to imagine?

HEAVENLY [*smiling cruelly*]: Why? I can't explain why.

ARTHUR: STOP IT! [*He raises his hands to his ears, then lowers them slowly.*] Don't smile at me that way!

HEAVENLY: Why did you cover your ears?

ARTHUR: I could hear them—yelling sissy at me—in the yard...

HEAVENLY: Oh.

MRS. CRITCHFIELD [*in the hall*]: Heavenly, dear!

HEAVENLY [*sotto voce*]: It's Mother. Please go now. She'll keep us forever and I've got to meet Dick.

[*Arthur doesn't move.*]

Will you please go?

MRS. CRITCHFIELD [*appearing in the hall with pitcher of lemonade*]: Heavenly, I'm going to drop these glasses! Ahthuh, how are you? Mmmm. [*She purrs dotingly as she extends her hand.*] I thought you young people might enjoy a little refreshment. It's just lemonade. [*She giggles foolishly and then notices the empty Coca-Cola bottles.*] Oh, dear, you've already had drinks?

HEAVENLY: I had a Coke. Ahthuh didn't want any.

MRS. CRITCHFIELD: Of course Ahthuh didn't. He's got too much

sense to poison himself with that stuff. I've heard it's habit-form-
ing. [*She sets down the pitcher.*] Heavenly, there's a little plate of
Aunt Lila's gingerbread cookies on the kitchen table. And you
might bring in a few napkins, dear.

HEAVENLY: Yes, mother. [*She crosses quickly out of the room.*]

MRS. CRITCHFIELD [*sitting with a benign purr*]: How is Mrs.
Shannon?

ARTHUR [*also sitting*]: Quite well, thank you.

MRS. CRITCHFIELD: That's good! —Mmmm—I suppose she
must have told you about the honor that she received last week?

ARTHUR: An honor?

MRS. CRITCHFIELD: Oh, my *yes*—yes, *indeed*! She was elected
Vice-Regent of the D.A. *Ahhh*! I was so pleased when her papers
went through. We need women of your mother's caliber so badly
in our patriotic societies. I happen to be serving as Regent this year.
I've served twice before in that capacity and once as Advisory
Regent and once as Sergeant-at-Arms! Mmmm. Club-work is so
absorbing. It makes one neglect other things. Such as books. What
do you think of the works of James Fenimore Cooper?

ARTHUR [*absently*]: Pardon?

MRS. CRITCHFIELD: James Fenimore Cooper—what do you
think of his works?

ARTHUR: Oh, yes—yes, indeed!

MRS. CRITCHFIELD [*brightly*]: Do you? I wondered if you did!

ARTHUR: Yes. . . .

MRS. CRITCHFIELD: Yes. . . .

[*There is a constrained silence. Mrs. Critchfield clears her throat and looks uneasily toward the rear door.*]

MRS. CRITCHFIELD: Pardon me a moment. I think Heavenly must be having some trouble in the kitchen.

[*Arthur rises as she goes out.*]

MRS. CRITCHFIELD [*from offstage*]: Heavenly, dear! Where *are* you, dear?

[*A terrible silence. She is heard running upstairs calling her daughter's name above. Arthur stands waiting in nervous misery till Mrs. Critchfield re-enters the room. She is completely unstrung by Heavenly's shocking flight, but with the invincible spirit of Colonel Wayne she resolves to carry it off as bravely as she is able, giving Arthur her most brilliant smile, a little tremulous at the corners.*]

Oh, dear, I'm afraid that Heavenly won't be able to come back in. The poor child is just prostrated and so I told her to go right on up to her bed and let me give you her excuses, Arthur. She didn't want to but when I saw how ill she was looking I—I just insisted! I told her that I was sure you would excuse her since she was feeling so badly.

ARTHUR [*embarrassed*]: Certainly, I— I'm dreadfully sorry. [*He moves toward the door.*] I hope it's nothing serious.

MRS. CRITCHFIELD: Oh, no, nothing serious, Arthur. She has such a nervous stomach, poor child. We call it the curse of the Critchfields.

ARTHUR: Oh. Please give her my sympathy. And tell her I hope she'll be well enough to go to the lawn party tomorrow.

MRS. CRITCHFIELD: Oh, she will! Arthur, I'm sure she will. Her nerves are just a little unstrung you know. She needs rest—I'll tell her that you excused her, Arthur.

ARTHUR: Thank you, Mrs. Critchfield. —Good night.

[*Arthur turns and goes into the hall. Mrs. Critchfield follows him.*]

MRS. CRITCHFIELD: Good night, Arthur. Give your mother my love. Tell her I do hope she'll be at the meeting tomorrow. Good night, Arthur. Good night—

[*The door is heard closing. Mrs. Critchfield comes slowly back into the living room with the brilliant, artificial smile still set on her face, her hand still raised in a parting gesture. The hand slowly falls and clasps her bosom. She simpers foolishly to herself, then gazes helplessly about the room. She lifts her hands to her lips with a breathless gasp, then her face puckers grotesquely and she begins to cry like a child as—*]

THE CURTAIN FALLS.

It is later that night. The stage is dark. Moonlight shines intermittently through the French window. Heavenly enters from the hall in pajamas. She walks slowly up to Colonel Wayne's portrait and speaks to it in a low voice.

HEAVENLY: Colonel Wayne! I'm sorry for what I said. I didn't mean it. I want you to forgive me! Please excuse me for disgracing your name! —If that's what I've done. I don't want to disgrace it—not any more than I have to. You know that as well as I do, Colonel Wayne! So please don't blame me too much! . . . I'm in an awful fix. I don't know what to do! . . . So why don't you come down off your horse and tell me instead of lookin' so big and important up there?

[*A light goes on in the hall. Mr. Critchfield enters in his dressing robe.*]

MR. CRITCHFIELD: Who's in there? Chicken?

HEAVENLY: Yes.

MR. CRITCHFIELD: What are you doing down here at three o'clock in the morning? I thought I heard you talking to somebody.

HEAVENLY: I was.

MR. CRITCHFIELD: Who was it? Who did you have in here at this hour? [*He turns on a table lamp.*]

HEAVENLY: Colonel Wayne.

MR. CRITCHFIELD: What?

HEAVENLY: Colonel Wayne! I was apologizing to him.

MR. CRITCHFIELD: Good Lord! [*He smiles a little.*] It's a long time since I heard you do that.

HEAVENLY: It's a long time since I told him to go back to Gettysburg.

MR. CRITCHFIELD: Did you?

HEAVENLY: Yes. Mother and I had a fight this afternoon. Didn't she tell you?

MR. CRITCHFIELD: Yes. We had a long talk tonight.

HEAVENLY: About—me?

MR. CRITCHFIELD: Yes. About you.

HEAVENLY: Dad, I— What's that you're drinking?

MR. CRITCHFIELD: Whiskey and soda. For my nerves.

HEAVENLY: I'd like to have one, too.

MR. CRITCHFIELD: Well—Heavenly, I—

HEAVENLY: Where is it? Behind the flour bin?

MR. CRITCHFIELD: You're psychic. [*She goes out to the kitchen; he calls to her.*] The soda's in the Frigidaire.

HEAVENLY [*calling*]: Yes, I know. [*In a moment she returns with a drink.*] You know, Daddy, this is the first drink we've ever had together.

MR. CRITCHFIELD: Yes, so it is. [*She sits on the sofa beside him.*]

HEAVENLY: It's stopped raining. The moon is coming out. [*She draws up her feet and leans against him.*] Daddy, are you very worried about me?

MR. CRITCHFIELD: Naturally I'm a little disturbed. But I'm not going to cross-examine you about your love affairs. I guess your mother's done plenty of that.

HEAVENLY: Everything's going to turn out all right. Dick's going to work for Mr. Kramer, and we're going to get married this summer. So there's nothing to worry about.

MR. CRITCHFIELD [*ruefully shaking his head*]: Chicken, chicken! Are you absolutely sure that you aren't talking through your little spring bonnet?

HEAVENLY [*hiding her face on his shoulder*]: No! I'm not!

MR. CRITCHFIELD [*stroking her head*]: Not even a little bit?

HEAVENLY [*abruptly straightening*]: Daddy! [*She looks at him with desperate pleading.*] Why is everything so crazy, so mixed up!? Why can't people be happy together? Why can't they want the same things, instead of—fighting and torturing and—hating each other—even when they're in love?!!

[*Mr. Critchfield gazes sadly, reflectively at the glittering ice in his glass.*]

MR. CRITCHFIELD: I guess those things are sort of natural phenomena. Like these spring storms we've been having. They do lots of damage. Bust the levees, wash out the bridges, destroy property and even kill people. What for? I don't know. [*He drains his glass and puts it on the table.*] I s'pose they're just the natural necessary parts of the changing season. . . . I'm getting sleepy.

HEAVENLY: Me, too. Let's tell Colonel Wayne good night!

[*Mr. Critchfield switches off the table lamp.*]

MR. CRITCHFIELD [*with grave humor*]: Honey, the Colonel and I haven't been on speakin' terms for about twenty years!

[*He puts his arm about her as they go out.*]

SLOW LIGHTS DOWN—END OF ACT TWO

ACT THREE

This scene should follow the dramaturgic pattern of Act One, starting lightly and rising through an emotional crescendo that culminates in the fight between Dick and Arthur and the outbreak of the storm.

The scene is the Lamphrey's lawn party. We are shown a secluded corner of the big lawn—a summer house or an arbor. Japanese lanterns are strung overhead and the set is backed by a trellis covered with flowering vines. In a prominent place is a small fountain with a little statue of Eros. Beside it is a stone bench, and at the right a punch stand with a cut-glass bowl and cups. For a touch of humor, the white-coated Negro servant is asleep, seated directly beneath the statue of Eros. The stringed orchestra from Memphis is playing. It stops—there is laughter and applause. In a moment Mrs. Lamphrey and three chaperones appear from the right.

MRS. DOWD: What do they call it? The Bag?

MRS. BUFORD: No, the Shag! I think it's horrid, don't you?

MRS. DOWD: I fail to see anything graceful about it. Now the old-fashioned cakewalk required some real skill in dancing—

MRS. LAMPHREY: Jackson! Wake up!

JACKSON: Yes'm, Mizz Lamphrey! Did I miss de contes'?

MRS. LAMPHREY: Yes, it's just over.

JACKSON: Doggone.

MRS. LAMPHREY: Pour the ladies some punch.

MRS. BUFORD: Oh, your moonvines are out.

MRS. LAMPHREY: Yes, everything's early this spring.

MRS. DOWD: So early.

MRS. ADAMS: Even Heavenly Critchfield's white organdy has come out a little earlier than usual this year.

MRS. BUFORD: It's fortunate that Esmeralda's so clever with the needle.

MRS. ADAMS: I don't believe they've bought a stitch of new clothes in five years.

MRS. BUFORD: What *are* their circumstances?

MRS. ADAMS: Desperate! Walter's been forced to discontinue their account.

MRS. BUFORD: Goodness!

MRS. LAMPHREY: They've been blacklisted for years by the Merchants' Credit Association. —It's a miracle to me how they're able to keep going. Mrs. Dowd— [*She offers her a glass.*]

MRS. DOWD: Thank you.

MRS. BUFORD: I pity Esmeralda but I've got no sympathy for Heavenly Critchfield.

MRS. ADAMS: She made a disgusting exhibition of herself.

MRS. LAMPHREY: Extremely! —Jackson, don't fill the glasses so full, they splash over.

MRS. ADAMS: Kicking up her skirts like a carnival dancer!

MRS. DOWD: Of course she's quite young—

MRS. ADAMS: Young nothing! She's twenty-three or four.

MRS. DOWD: And with such a fine old family as the Waynes and the Critchfields—

MRS. ADAMS: She'll be ostracized, mark my word! Not a decent boy in town'll be seen with her. She'll end up sitting on a front porch.

MRS. BUFORD: Or going with drummers!

MRS. DOWD: Well, at present the Shannon boy seems to be quite devoted.

MRS. LAMPHREY: I wonder how Mrs. Shannon feels about that?

MRS. ADAMS: Strongly opposed, of course. [*Sotto voce.*] Have you heard what Tom Newby told his mother this morning about what he saw at Moon Lake?

MRS. LAMPHREY: Goodness, no! What?

MRS. ADAMS: Heavenly and the Miles boy were seen coming out of a tourist cabin—

MRS. LAMPHREY: Tourist cabin!

MRS. ADAMS: Yes, at about two o'clock this morning!

MRS. LAMPHREY: Why didn't you tell me before? Oh, my Lord!

MRS. DOWD: I think it's unfair to repeat that kind of gossip.

MRS. ADAMS: It's been substantiated. And of course I've thought right along—

MRS. LAMPHREY: Oh, I did, *too*. But after *this*!

MRS. ADAMS: I think some definite measures should be taken to express our feelings. After all she's associating with our sons and daughters.

MRS. LAMPHREY: Oh, my goodness, yes! Susan has very little to do with her but *still*—

MRS. ADAMS: I've warned Henry.

MRS. BUFORD: Annabelle and John Dudley dropped her in high school. They say she's so uppity and independent that—

MRS. DOWD: Mrs. Lamphrey!

MRS. LAMPHREY: Yes?

MRS. DOWD: Such delicious punch!

MRS. ADAMS: Oh, yes, isn't it though? Are those rain clouds?

MRS. LAMPHREY: If it does rain, we'll simply move the pahty indoors.

MRS. BUFORD: Look! She's coming across the lawn with your son.

MRS. ADAMS [*alarmed*]: Henry?

MRS. LAMPHREY: And Arthur Shannon!

MRS. BUFORD: I wouldn't be surprised if—

MRS. LAMPHREY: Shhh!

[*Heavenly enters with Arthur and Henry. The men are in tuxedos. Heavenly is a radiant dream-like vision in her white organdy under the soft-colored lanterns and with the background of poignant string music. She is bearing a frosted, candle-lit cake which she has just won at the dance.*]

HEAVENLY: Oh, I'm still out of breath! Hank, did you get the cake knife?

HENRY: You bet.

HEAVENLY: Thanks. Hello. [*To the ladies in general.*] Can't I offer you a slice, Mrs. Lamphrey? Mrs. Adams—Mrs. Buford—Mrs. Dowd?

[*They decline, Mrs. Dowd politely, but the others with noticeable coolness.*]

Hank, will you?

HENRY: You bet.

MRS. ADAMS [*quickly*]: Henry, will you please get me my shawl from the house?

MRS. LAMPHREY: There's a wind coming up. I should have known better than to give an outdoor party at this time of year.

MRS. BUFORD: Such peculiar weather! Torrential rains and days like midsummer! I wonder if the levee's in danger?

MRS. ADAMS: It is north of here. We've moved all our furniture upstairs and the quarters have simply cleared out. [*She turns to her son who has not moved.*] —Henry! Right away, dear! —Mrs. Buford, I want you to meet those Tupelo girls, they're lovely, so nice and *refined*!

[*Mrs. Adams, Mrs. Buford and Mrs. Lamphrey go out right.*]

MRS. DOWD [*to Heavenly*]: Congratulations, dear. I enjoyed your dancing so much and your little white dress is divine. I'm going to make a special note of it in my column tomorrow! [*She kisses Heavenly quickly and goes out.*]

HEAVENLY: I don't know which I'd rather be, snubbed or pitied. [*To Jackson.*] Jackson, have you got anything in the punch?

JACKSON: No, Ma'am, Mizz Lamphrey gib me obstructions not to put in a drap.

HEAVENLY: Not even for the gentlemen?

JACKSON: Well, Mr. Lamphrey, he sez, I should keep dis bottle hid unduh de napkin case some ob de *olduh* gennulmens ast for it an'—

HEAVENLY: Give it here!

JACKSON: An' den I was to gib em a small amount an'—

HEAVENLY: Let me have it!

JACKSON: An' no more!

HEAVENLY [*wresting it from him*]: I'll do the mixing myself, you might give me too much. Arthur? Oh, I forgot—you never take stimulants after six-thirty.

ARTHUR: Tonight I'll make an exception.

HEAVENLY: Marvelous! —Jackson, if you snitch on me I'll get Dick Miles to skin you alive! —Well, that's *quite* an exception! Are you planning to do some desperate deed tonight?

MRS. LAMPHREY [*offstage*]: Jackson!

JACKSON: Yes'm, Mizz Lamphrey?

MRS. LAMPHREY [*appearing, nervous*]: Jackson, you'll have to help clear off the table. I'm afraid it's going to rain before long and I want you to get all the linen and silver inside. Heavenly, dear, we'll leave you in chahge of the punch! [*Mrs. Lamphrey exits with Jackson.*]

[*There is a constrained silence between Heavenly and Arthur. He stands by the fountain with his back to her. She seats herself on the stone bench—suddenly laughs.*]

ARTHUR: What are you laughing at?

HEAVENLY: Oh, nothing. —I didn't think I'd ever see you after last night.

ARTHUR: Neither did I.

HEAVENLY: It was sweet of you to fo'give me. In fact it was noble.

ARTHUR: Being noble is one of my worst afflictions.

HEAVENLY: I don't think so. —I know my behavior is awful.

ARTHUR: The worst thing about your behavior is its complete inconsistency.

HEAVENLY: Yes?

ARTHUR: Last night you expressed a desperate fear of being left on a porch swing. And yet right afterwards you do things that are perfectly calculated to bring that about!

HEAVENLY: I know, I know! I'm a fool! —*Look!*

ARTHUR: What?

HEAVENLY [*softly*]: It's the first lightnin' bug!

[*Pause. Music is heard.*]

HEAVENLY: Wonder what makes 'em go off and on like that? —Did you take any science courses at Oxfo'd? I took geology my third yeah at high.

ARTHUR [*coldly*]: Did you really?

HEAVENLY: Yes. We used to go out on field expeditions they called 'em, collectin' fossils an' things.

ARTHUR: That must've been nice!

HEAVENLY: Yes, an' just think! —Someday we'll be fossils, too. They'll dig us up an' say, "Gosh what long legs that girl had!"— or "Didn't he have nice ears!" —An' that's all they'll know about us, I suppose.

ARTHUR: I suppose so.

HEAVENLY: It won't matter who we got married to or whether we lived to be old or died young. They won't care; it won't make any difference to them. We'll just be little marks on a piece of rock. Or maybe not even that much. —Does it make you feel sad?

ARTHUR: No. —Are you trying to make conversation?

HEAVENLY: Um-hmm.

ARTHUR: What for?

HEAVENLY: It's part of my social training.

ARTHUR: You needn't.

HEAVENLY: You're still mad about last night. I thought you accepted my apologies over the phone.

ARTHUR: I knew you were lying over the phone.

HEAVENLY: You mean about my nervous indigestion?

ARTHUR: Yes, your mother came back to me with that same ridiculous story after calling your name all over the house.

HEAVENLY: Mother's a terrible fool sometimes.

ARTHUR: I felt sorry for her. I could understand your wanting to hurt me—because after all you've done that repeatedly in the past—but it did surprise me a little that you'd be willing to cause your mother such embarrassment.

HEAVENLY: You said I was cruel before.

ARTHUR: I said unconsciously cruel. But what you did last night was on purpose.

HEAVENLY: It really wasn't on purpose. You made me so mad, what you said about Dick an' me, that when mother sent me out for the napkins—well I just kept going till I'd gotten six blocks from the house. An' then it was too late to go back so I went to meet Dick an' he took me out to Moon Lake.

ARTHUR [*coldly*]: Oh.

HEAVENLY: But I didn't have any fun. I kept thinking about what I'd done all the time an' I really did feel sorry, Ahthuh. I wasn't lyin' when I told you that over the phone.— Now do you fo'give me?

ARTHUR: I don't think it particularly matters whether I forgive you or not.

HEAVENLY: I think it does. I think I should like you an awful lot if you'd just be a little more human.

ARTHUR: What is being human?

HEAVENLY: You see you don't even know!

[*Henry enters.*]

HENRY: Heavenly, can I speak to you about something?

HEAVENLY: Sure you can, honey.

HENRY: I mean alone, Heavenly.

ARTHUR: Excuse me. [*He exits stage left.*]

HEAVENLY: Gosh, Hank, you look awful serious, honey! What's wrong?

HENRY: I thought you oughta know that Tom Newby's been talking about you to people. He told his mother and she's gone an' told Mizz Lamphrey an' Mizz Lamphrey's told Fanny and—and—

HEAVENLY: Told what?

HENRY: Tom Newby said—he said he saw you an' Dick Miles comin' out of a tourist cabin last night.

HEAVENLY: Oh.

HENRY: At Moon Lake, he said, and it was two o'clock in the morning! Of cou'se I know he's lyin' but—

HEAVENLY: What if it's true? [*She speaks violently.*] Whose business is it anyhow? What right have they got to—!

HENRY: I know but some of the old ladies, I heard 'em talking when I brought Mother's shawl— Mrs. Adams, she said she thought you ought to be—ostracized! What's that?

HEAVENLY: Ostracized? Did she say that?

HENRY: Yes. Is that what they did to that—you know—that girl across the Sunflower River?

HEAVENLY: No. Honey, you run back to the dance.

HENRY: That stinkin' polecat, Newby, I'm gonna push his face in! But I thought you oughta know first.

HEAVENLY: Thanks, honey.

HENRY [*blurting this out*]: Heavenly, you're—you're beautiful! I wish that I was Dick Miles! [*He goes quickly out right.*]

[*Heavenly laughs wildly.*]

ARTHUR [*returning*]: What's so hilariously funny?

HEAVENLY: He wished he was Dick Miles! Oh, God, it's beautiful, isn't it? [*Then she speaks furiously.*] I'm going to tell those bitches where to head in!

ARTHUR [*catching her wrist*]: Heavenly!

HEAVENLY [*quietly after a moment*]: Thanks. It's good you did that. Sometimes I don't think what I'm doing.

ARTHUR: You never do. You've got the instinct for self-destruction.

HEAVENLY: Is that what it is?

ARTHUR: Yes.

HEAVENLY: I probably got it from Colonel Wayne. You know he led the charge up Cemetery Hill.

ARTHUR: And you want to do the same thing?

HEAVENLY: If I have to.

ARTHUR: Right in the teeth of their guns with the odds all against you?

HEAVENLY: Why not? I wish I was ten years younger, I'd like to kick Tom Newby so hard he couldn't sit down for a month. I did that once about ten years ago and it's given me satisfaction ever since.

ARTHUR: What's he done?

HEAVENLY: Snitched on me, same as he did last time!

ARTHUR: About what?

HEAVENLY: Oh, you'll hear soon enough. The whole town will. —[*She continues, frightened.*] Mrs. Adams said I ought to be ostracized. Do you know what that means?

ARTHUR: Yes. It's what happens to rebels.

HEAVENLY: I don't give a damn. —It's the Pink Lady Waltz! Let's dance!

ARTHUR: No.

HEAVENLY: Why not?

ARTHUR: I'm not a good dancer

HEAVENLY: You're good enough. Come on! [*She takes his arm.*]

ARTHUR: I'd rather not dance.

HEAVENLY: Oh, you're ashamed to dance with me? It might damage your good reputation.

ARTHUR: You know it's not that.

HEAVENLY: What is it then?

ARTHUR: I'm very uncomfortable when we're dancing together.

HEAVENLY: Why are you?

ARTHUR: Sometimes it hurts a man to be close to a woman— just so close and not any closer than that.

HEAVENLY: Oh! [*Pause.*] I wouldn't expect you to say a thing like that.

ARTHUR: Why not? Isn't that part of what you call being human?

HEAVENLY: Yes. That's why it surprised me so much.

[*There is a murmur of wind and a glimmer of lighting on the cyclorama.*]

Lightning. It's going to storm.

ARTHUR: Yes. I guess that's why the Little God's so excited. —He likes spring storms.

HEAVENLY: Does he?

ARTHUR: Yes. They've so much in common, you know. They're both so damn cruel—reckless and destructive!

HEAVENLY: Like me. Is that what you mean?

ARTHUR: Yes. I believe the Greeks were laughing when they made him the Little God. Eros is really the biggest god of them all. He's the one that's got thunderbolts!

HEAVENLY: What did you call him?

ARTHUR: Pardon me! I thought that you knew each other! —This is Eros, the Little God of Love, Miss Heavenly Critchfield!

HEAVENLY: How do you do? [*She laughs.*] I've always called him Cupid.

ARTHUR: Yes, that's the usual misconception. People think he's a cute, chubby little fellow with dimples and curly locks—but they're fooling themselves because he's really a monster!

HEAVENLY: Is he?

[*The scene plays very fast from here to Dick's entrance.*]

ARTHUR: Yes. Can't you feel him breathing fire in your face?

[*The wind rises. The orchestra is playing a fast waltz.*]

HEAVENLY: No. Not in mine.

ARTHUR: You're lucky, Miss Critchfield— Luckier than I. — What're you laughing at?

HEAVENLY: At you! You make such fancy speeches!

ARTHUR: You think I'm ludicrous, don't you?

HEAVENLY: No. I think you're a fake! [*Pause.*]

ARTHUR [*quietly*]: A fake?

HEAVENLY: Yes, an absolute fake!

ARTHUR: You're right. I *am* a fake. I haven't got a real bone in my body.

HEAVENLY: I know you haven't.

ARTHUR: You know it surprises me sometimes to see that I even make a shadow in the light. It's a wonder the light doesn't shine right through me like it does through a cloud of dust in the road.

HEAVENLY: That's funny— I have the same feeling about you.

ARTHUR: I know that you do. [*He crosses to her.*] But just once I'd like to touch you and make you feel I'm alive.

HEAVENLY [*away*]: What?

ARTHUR: Because then maybe I *would* be alive. You could give me back what you took away from me—that afternoon when you laughed at me in the recess yard!

HEAVENLY: What I took away from you? Then?

ARTHUR: Yes! You took away everything!

HEAVENLY: Arthur—

ARTHUR: After that I wasn't real anymore.

HEAVENLY: You're drunk.

ARTHUR: No, I was just the shadow of something and that's all I've been ever since.

HEAVENLY: What could I do about that?

ARTHUR: You could—you could *love* me—make me sure again I'm alive!

HEAVENLY: Oh, I see. [*She laughs.*] You mean what Henry meant when he said he wished that he was Dick Miles— Only you dress it up in prettier speeches, don't you? Here. Take the rest of the whiskey. Go cross the Sunflower River and get yourself one of those bright-skinned women they've got over there. They're marvelous at—at proving you're alive, if that's what you're worried about!

ARTHUR: You don't understand.

HEAVENLY: Oh, yes I do.

ARTHUR: I want you to marry me, Heavenly!

HEAVENLY: What? —You didn't say that! [*Pause.*]

ARTHUR: Will you? Will you, Heavenly?

HEAVENLY [*very softly*]: I don't know. I don't see how I could.

ARTHUR: You couldn't love me?

HEAVENLY: How should I know? You've never even kissed me?

ARTHUR [*importunately*]: May I? Will you let me?

HEAVENLY: Oh, you're so funny, Arthur! [*She laughs.*] I gave you every chance last night an' you started to read mode'n verse.

ARTHUR: I couldn't help it! —I've always run away from things that I wanted.

HEAVENLY: I don't know what to think, what to say! Everything's going so fast! —You know I can feel the earth moving! It's going a thousand miles a minute, it's spinning round and round!

ARTHUR: That's the wind!

HEAVENLY: I know, I know, but it's making me dizzy! [*She sinks down.*]

FANNY [*offstage*]: Oh, Heavenly! Heavenly!

HEAVENLY: You see how fast it's going? We can't be still for a minute! [*She answers Fanny.*] Yes?

[*Fanny enters followed by Dick Miles.*]

FANNY: Oh, here you are, still having a *tête-à-tête* with the guest of honor! —There's another gentleman to see you!

HEAVENLY: Dick!

DICK: Scuse me for bustin' in, but I got something important to talk to you about.

HEAVENLY: How could you come here like this? You look like you've been having a mud-fight!

DICK: I have! I've been rasseling the river.

FANNY: Oh, we'll excuse your appearance. [*To Heavenly.*] We all know that Dick Miles is too big for social conventions.

DICK: That's right.

FANNY: [*to Arthur*]: Have you all met each othuh?

ARTHUR [*coldly*]: I've had the pleasure quite some time ago.

DICK: Sure. [*He grins*] Do you still read *The Wizard of Oz*?

ARTHUR [*furiously*]: No. Do you still enjoy taking advantage of your—your physical superiority? Do you still—

HEAVENLY: Arthur!

FANNY: Arthur, that's my favorite piece they're playing!

ARTHUR: Excuse me. [*He goes off with Fanny.*]

HEAVENLY: Now are you satisfied? You've made a beautiful scene!

DICK: Sorry. I had to see you. This is important, honey.

HEAVENLY: Important? You couldn't tell me tomorrow?

DICK: No. I'm not going to be here tomorrow.

HEAVENLY: —What?

DICK: We're leaving town.

HEAVENLY: We? —Thanks for telling me.

DICK: I mean it this time. Absolutely no doggin'. I been to Friar's Point—that's where I picked up this mud I got on me. [*He places his hands on her shoulders.*] Heavenly, I've got a job on the Government levee project.

HEAVENLY: No!

DICK: I've already signed the papers. I can show 'em to you.

HEAVENLY [*desperately*]: No, Dick!

DICK: Huh?

HEAVENLY: You can't do a thing like that to me!

DICK: A thing like what?

HEAVENLY: You can't walk out on me, Dick!

DICK: I'm not walking out on you, honey. I'm takin' you with me.

HEAVENLY: Me? On a government levee project?

DICK: Sure, a man's allowed to be married.

HEAVENLY: Is he? I didn't know that. I thought those levee workers lived with niggers.

DICK: Heavenly—

HEAVENLY: That's what I heard. I heard they kept colored women in their shacks with them.

DICK [*disgustedly*]: I knew you'd take it like that.

HEAVENLY: Dick, you've got a job here.

DICK: In the drugstore.

HEAVENLY: No. In Mr. Kramer's cotton office.

DICK: That's absolutely out. I won't take it.

HEAVENLY: Dad's made him promise. It's a sure thing.

DICK: No! I won't take it! [*He catches her shoulders.*] Honey, it takes a pair of boots and a flannel shirt to make me feel like a man. I'm sick of bath salts and spirits of ammonia. An' I wouldn't like cotton much better. Cotton's soft. It's fuzzy stuff that sticks to your fingers. I wouldn't like that. I want to get my hands on something hard and tough that fights back, like the river. When you're fighting a river you're fighting something your size. Don't you see? They've put out flood warnings up at Friar's Point. She's rose six feet since morning. Fifty-nine, that's flood stage, and God only knows when she'll stop. They're fighting like crazy to hold her back but she keeps on coming, big an' yellow an' daring 'em all to try an' make her stay put. She'll win this time maybe. Push right through their sandbags an' run 'em out of the county, tearin' down sharecroppers houses an' drownin' the stock. If the people are lucky they'll climb on top of their roofs an' we'll take 'em off in boats. But some of 'em won't be lucky. Ole Mammies with breakbone fever ain't good at roof climbing. The river'll catch 'em at night an' they won't have a chance. But maybe next time we'll win. We'll catch her an' tame her an' make her stay in her place. That's a big job, honey, the kind of job that I want! [*Pause.*]

HEAVENLY: More than you want me? That much?

DICK: I want you and the job both.

HEAVENLY: You can't have both. I can't live like that, in a shack on the river— You can't ask me to.

DICK: Well, that's what I'm asking. You'll have to go with me or—

HEAVENLY: Oh, it's an ultimatum.

DICK: You can call it that.

HEAVENLY: In other words you're tired of me, you've had enough!

DICK: Come off you high horse!

HEAVENLY: I've still got some pride, some self-respect!

DICK: You've still got your ancestry, your marvelous ancestry! You can't forget about that!

HEAVENLY: I can't forget that I'm decent!

DICK: But you can forget Moon Lake last night, or yesterday up on the hill? You can forget those things in about twenty minutes and throw it up to me that I'm not good enough for you?

HEAVENLY: It's you that's forgetting, not me. Every spring it's the same. You get a spell like this an' later you come to your senses.

DICK: You got around me last spring. Made me stay.

HEAVENLY: Don't you remember *how* I made you stay?

DICK: Yes, I remember how.

HEAVENLY: It wasn't easy for me to do that. I thought it meant something.

DICK: It did.

HEAVENLY: Not to you or you wouldn't be throwing me over.

DICK: Honey, I'm *not* throwing you over.

HEAVENLY: You are. You're throwing me over—you want me to be like Agnes Peabody next door—a front porch girl! She sits on the front porch in her best dress and the men walk by in the evening and tip their hats and keep right on walking. People remember how she went out all the time with a boy that's left town. Now she just sits on the front porch waiting! —waiting for nothing, getting to be an old maid! —That's what you want to happen to me!

DICK: No, honey, you know better than that.

HEAVENLY: How should I know any better?

DICK: I asked you to go with me.

HEAVENLY: Yes, you asked me to go with you! And you knew damn well that I couldn't!

DICK: I knew you loved me. I mean I thought I knew you loved me.

HEAVENLY: Oh. And now you think different. You think that I've done what I've done because I'm just naturally rotten. Is that what you think?

DICK: No. Let it go.

HEAVENLY: I won't. We'll have this out now.

DICK: All right. You can do what you please but I'm goin'.

HEAVENLY [*her voice breaking*]: Then it's all finished then. You can go, you don't have to come back. I'd rather sit out on a front porch the rest of my life than ever see you again. —But I won't be sitting on the front porch! I'll take Arthur! He told me he wanted me just now, before you came butting in!

DICK: Heavenly!—

HEAVENLY: Go away!

DICK: You don't want me to! Lissen, Heavenly!

HEAVENLY: No!

DICK: Have you ever spent a night on the river, honey?

HEAVENLY: Let go of me!

[*He forces her down on the bench and holds her against him.*]

DICK: Have you ever spent a night on a river barge, honey? That clean wet smell of the woods and maybe a hole in the roof you can see the stars through? Katydids hummin' an' bullfrogs off in the shallows. That dark warm smell of the water real close an' the sound that it makes that's so quiet it's sca'cely a sound, just a big, big black-ness movin' around you, an' up on the deck a nigger pickin' a fiddle an' singin' an ole river song, an' that lazy soft rise an' fall of the water under the boat an' the lightnin' bugs blinkin' way off over there on the flat cotton fields or down in the cypress break an' that wild coon laughter all of a sudden comin' up out of the dark where they're makin' love on the levee—like cryin' almost—an' then not a thing anymore but that slow slappin'-slap of the water . . .

HEAVENLY: Dick—

DICK: I've spent nights like that on the river! By myself or with a bunch of fellows—but never with a girl I loved!

HEAVENLY [breaking away]: Dick, it's impossible!

[The wind has risen. They have to shout above it.]

DICK [trying to kiss her again]: No, it isn't!

HEAVENLY: Stop it!

DICK [slowly]: You mean you won't go?

HEAVENLY [brokenly]: You know that I couldn't stand it.

DICK: You could if you loved me.

HEAVENLY: If I loved you, if I loved you! —All that you think of is self, self, self!

DICK: It's you that don't think of anything but self!

HEAVENLY: Oh, Dick! Don't say anymore tonight, please don't!

DICK: I got nothing more to say.

HEAVENLY: They're all going in the house, it's going to storm. — I can't stay out here any longer, Dick.

DICK: I'm not keeping you.

HEAVENLY [*catching his arm*]: Oh, Dick — don't, don't! *Please* don't!

[*Arthur enters right.*]

ARTHUR [*drunkenly*]: Heavenly, where are you, Heavenly?

DICK: What do *you* want?

ARTHUR: I want to take her inside!

DICK: You take her nowhere, Sonny. She's going with me.

HEAVENLY: Dick, don't make another scene!

ARTHUR: Why don't you leave her alone? You can't marry her, all you can do is make her talked about. [*He's in a drunken rage.*] You know what they say about the two of you—do you know?

HEAVENLY [*screaming*]: Arthur! Go 'way! Go back to the house!

ARTHUR: They say she's your mistress! They say—

[*Dick knocks him down—then jerks him up, shakes him, and flings him down again—Heavenly tries to stop him.*]

HEAVENLY: Dick! You'll kill him—he's drunk!

DICK: —I didn't hurt him.

HEAVENLY [*bends over Arthur*]: You did.

DICK: All right. You stay here with him. Wrap him up in tissue paper and send him back to Mama with my regards!

[*He starts off.*]

HEAVENLY [*rising*]: Dick!—

DICK: Good-bye!

HEAVENLY: Call me tomorrow! You'll call me, won't you?

DICK: Good-bye, Heavenly! [*He exits.*]

[*She runs after him a short distance, calling his name wildly. She stops, sobbing aloud. As the storm breaks, she turns and runs toward the house.*

The Japanese lanterns flicker and sway in the wind. The cable that supports them snaps and they are blown tumbling across the stage. There is the sound of branches thrashing, a cacophony of noises from the suddenly disrupted lawn party, and, through it all, expressing the frenzied spirit of the scene, are heard the distant strains of the waltz, fast and feverishly gay. There is a crash of thunder. —Arthur rises, staggering. He goes over to the statue of Eros. He stands unsteadily before it, laughing louder and louder as the storm's fury increases— There is a vivid flash of lightning and then complete darkness.]

THE CURTAIN FALLS

The scene is the Carnegie Public Library of Port Tyler. The set is furnished with a yellow oak desk, a table, a chair, and a newspaper and magazine rack. A green-shaded bulb is suspended over the librarian's desk and a small lamp rests on the table. Against the back wall or on the bulletin board are travel posters of "Beautiful Switzerland" and "Romantic Italy." A sign on the desk says "Quiet Please" In the middle of the back wall is an opaque glass-paned door marked "Stacks." Hertha is seated at the desk in a prim gray smock and glasses. She looks tired and strained. Enter Mrs. Kramer, a prim-looking matron.

MRS. KRAMER [*marching to the desk*]: I found this book in my daughter's bedroom!

HERTHA: Yes?

MRS. KRAMER: I don't think books like this should be exposed on the shelves.

HERTHA: It happens to be a private copy of my own.

MRS. KRAMER: Well, how did she get it?

HERTHA: She saw me reading it and asked to read it herself.

MRS. KRAMER: Oh. It may be fit reading for an older person, but Dorothea's sixteen. So far I've managed to keep her mind entirely free of—of sordid things such as—

HERTHA: This book? There's nothing sordid about this book, Mrs. Kramer—nothing whatsoever!

MRS. KRAMER: Oh, isn't there? I always consult Reverend Hooker about my child's reading matter— When I showed him this book he turned directly to this passage and asked me if it was the sort of thing I wanted my child's mind infected with—here it is— [*She reads a verse of love poetry.*]

> What lips my lips have kissed, and where and why,
> I have forgotten, and what arms have lain
> Under my head till morning—

HERTHA [*snatching the book*]:   You can't read it like that, Mrs. Kramer!

MRS. KRAMER: No?

HERTHA [*repeating the passage with feeling*]:

> What lips my lips have kissed, and where and why,
> I have forgotten, and what arms have lain
> Under my head till morning; but the rain
> Is full of ghosts tonight, that tap and sigh
> Upon the glass and listen for reply:
>
> And in my heart there stirs a quiet pain
> For unremembered lads that not again
> Will turn to me at midnight with a cry.

[*She fixes her eyes on Mrs. Kramer and recites the rest of the poem from memory.*]

> Thus in the winter stands the lonely tree,
> Nor knows what birds have vanished one by one,
> Yet knows its boughs more silent than before:
> I cannot say what loves have come and gone;
> I only know that summer sang in me
> A little while, that in me sings no more.

Now don't you like it better?

MRS. KRAMER: No. I think it's outrageous. Next time Dorothea wants a book, please give her one of the Alcott series.

HERTHA: Isn't Dorothea rather old for the Alcott series?

MRS. KRAMER [*furiously*]: She's not too old for innocence, thank heavens, and she's not too young for common sense— Good night, Miss Neilson. [*She marches out.*]

[*Hertha opens the book— Music comes through the opened windows from the Lamphrey's party. Hertha closes the book, rises quickly and shuts the window. She returns slowly to the desk. After a moment, Miss Schlagmann comes out of the door marked "Stacks."*]

MISS SCHLAGMANN: Oh, it's so close in here. Why did you close that window?

HERTHA: It's going to storm.

MISS SCHLAGMANN: We might as well leave it open till it rains in. [*She goes over and raises the window. Music enters again and there is the glimmer of lightning outside.*] Listen! You can hear the music from the Lamphrey's lawn party!

HERTHA: Yes.

MISS SCHLAGMANN: They've got Japanese lanterns strung all over the place. —It looks like fairyland.

HERTHA: Yes.

MISS SCHLAGMANN: Oh, dear—young people have such a good

time, don't they? How would you like to go to the movies with me next Saturday night, Hertha?

HERTHA: Thank you, but—

MISS SCHLAGMANN: It'll be my treat this time! —They have that Tyrone Power picture. And they always have the Tarzan serial.

HERTHA: Do they?

MISS SCHLAGMANN [*laughing sharply*]: They're so absurd! But they *are* exciting! At the end of the last one he and the girl were locked in a dungeon with lions! —[*She laughs.*] But I suppose they'll manage to get out somehow.

HERTHA: Yes. [*She smiles slightly.*]

MISS SCHLAGMANN: They're obliged to get out. That's only the sixteenth chapter and there's supposed to be thirty-two— If they killed 'em off now they wouldn't have anything to put in the other sixteen.

HERTHA: No. Not unless they had a very elaborate funeral.

MISS SCHLAGMANN: You don't like the movies?

HERTHA: Sometimes. I liked that last one of Greta Garbo's.

MISS SCHLAGMANN: Her things are always so morbid or sordid or something!

HERTHA [*laughing*]: That's twice this evening that I've been accused of having sordid predilections.

MISS SCHLAGMANN [*starting back to the "Stacks," she pauses at*

111

the desk]: Here's something *I* like—jonquils! —They're so fresh looking! [*She sniffs them delicately, then exits through the rear door.*]

[*Hertha reopens the book of poems. The muted strains of the Strauss waltz from the Lamphrey's are heard. Suddenly she throws down the book. She rushes to the window and slams it shut. She raises one hand to her lips in an almost terrified gesture, then touches her forehead and returns slowly to the desk. She clears her throat and straightens things on the desk with a furious but aimless haste— A young couple enters—Mabel and Ralph.*]

MABEL: It would have to rain.

RALPH: Jeez, what a wind's comin' up.

MABEL: I'm scared sick a' storms. Specially when it thunders. Ralph! [*She clings to him.*]

RALPH: Aw, honey, thunder can't hurtcha.

MABEL [*giggling*]: She's lookin' at us.

RALPH: What do we care, huh?

HERTHA [*rising and approaching them stiffly*]: This room is for reading purposes only.

RALPH: What're we doin'?

HERTHA: You're creating a disturbance.

RALPH: A disturbance, huh?

HERTHA: Yes!

RALPH: Can't we even carry on a little conversation in here?

HERTHA: Conversation, yes, but not disorderly behavior.

MABEL [*rising indignantly*]: He's my fiancé! —Ralph, let's get out of this place! [*She crosses to the door.*] I'd rather get pneumonia than be bawled out by that cranky old maid!

[*As they go out Ralph laughs rudely. Hertha stands erect till they have gone—then suddenly covers her face— She quickly lowers her hands as the inner door opens and Miss Schlagmann comes back out with an armful of books.*]

MISS SCHLAGMANN: I thought I heard some loud talk in here.

HERTHA: That boy and girl were in here again. The ones that were necking in here last week.

MISS SCHLAGMANN: Oh!

HERTHA: I asked them to please be quiet and they were horribly rude to me.

MISS SCHLAGMANN: I'm going to speak to Mr. Gillam. She works there, at the hosiery counter. I think—being a vestryman of St. George's—he'd like to know how one of his salesgirls spends her free time, making a public show of herself and her common affairs.

HERTHA: No. Don't. —He might discharge her.

MISS SCHLAGMANN: He should.

HERTHA: No. It wasn't anything at all. I haven't been feeling well and they made me nervous. —They called me a—

MISS SCHLAGMANN: Called you what?

HERTHA [*averting her face*]: A—cranky old maid.

MISS SCHLAGMANN [*furious*]: Well, what preposterous—!

HERTHA: No, they were right! That's what I am now!

MISS SCHLAGMANN [*shocked*]: Hertha! What's wrong with you child?

HERTHA [*crossing behind the desk*]: Nothing. I'm nervous.

MISS SCHLAGMANN: I'm going to report this to Mr. Gillam.

HERTHA: Please don't. [*She takes a handkerchief from a drawer and turns her back.*]

MISS SCHLAGMANN: Hertha, I'm afraid you're getting run down again this spring. You'd better take a week off.

HERTHA: I'm all right. It's just nervousness. [*She turns and sits down rigidly at the desk.*] —Maybe I'm losing my mind.

MISS SCHLAGMANN: Don't be absurd!

HERTHA: Lots of girls do at my age. Twenty-eight. Lots of them get *dementia praecox* at about that age, especially when they're not married. I've read about it. They get morbid and everything excites them and they think they're being persecuted by people. I'm getting like that.

MISS SCHLAGMANN: You are not! [*She speaks gently.*] I know what's wrong with you, Hertha. It's that Shannon boy— Isn't it now?

HERTHA [*with effort*]: —Yes.

MISS SCHLAGMANN: I knew that was it. You took him too seriously. I could have told you right at the start he wouldn't do anything but make you unhappy. I had him spotted. Attractive and intelligent and all that but selfish right to the core. One of these spoiled millionaire's children. They're all the same way. They think the whole earth was created for their entertainment. [*She returns several books to a shelf.*] You get him out of your mind.

HERTHA: I can't. [*She looks almost wildly about the room.*] He's the first man that ever looked at me twice. And I can't stop thinking about him. Even at night. I haven't been sleeping.

MISS SCHLAGMANN: I know you haven't. You need a change of scene.

HERTHA: Oh, no, I can't stop working!

MISS SCHLAGMANN: You can if it's necessary to stop a nervous breakdown.

HERTHA: It wouldn't help. I've got to keep busy. You see when I'm not busy I— [*She presses her hands to her temples.*] Why doesn't God have a little mercy on people like me? You go to church, Miss Schlagmann, you teach Sunday school. You ought to know. Why doesn't God have a little mercy on people like me? Ask Him that the next time you go to St. George's. Tell Him He shouldn't give homely girls the same feelings that He gives the pretty ones. Tell Him that. Tell Him it isn't fair to let the homely girls fall in love with men that don't care!

[*Miss Schlagmann makes a gesture of shocked pity; she bites her lips and fumbles at the silver cross suspended over her flat bosom.*]

MISS SCHLAGMANN [*hesitantly*]: Hertha, I wish you would go with me to some of the Lenten services next week at St. George's. It's going to be Holy Week. Our Lord's Passion, you know. — Don't you suppose He went through moments like these that you're going through—when He suffered and doubted and—prepared His soul for climbing up that hill and being nailed on a cross between two thieves!

HERTHA [*slowly*]: Well, if He did, He ought to know what it's like and He ought to have some pity! I can't go on living much longer in this kind of vacuum. It isn't fair to make me, it isn't fair!

MISS SCHLAGMANN: Lots of things aren't fair, but we've got to put up with them just the same. That's life.

HERTHA [*fiercely*]: I'm tired of hearing people say, "That's life!"

MISS SCHLAGMANN: I know. I've been through the same thing. It's a sort of an emotional crisis that all of us have to go through that don't get married and haven't the courage for anything else. After a while it gets better. You find out that you can put those feelings into other things.

HERTHA [*bitterly*]: Yes. Sublimation. Choir singing and raising petunias. I don't want that.

MISS SCHLAGMANN: Hertha!

HERTHA: There ought to be something else! [*She speaks almost to herself.*] A straight line upwards to someplace nobody's ever been yet. I told him that and he laughed, Arthur did. He said I meant 'Paradise'—but I didn't. I don't know what I meant. —Why doesn't your fashionable Episcopal minister at St. George's try to figure that out instead of worrying about how he's going to finance the new pipe organ?

MISS SCHLAGMANN: Don't talk like that!

HERTHA: I know, I know. I ought to keep my mouth shut. That's what's expected of me. But I can't anymore. I'm sick of it.

[*Agnes Peabody enters.*]

MISS SCHLAGMANN: It's Agnes Peabody. You'd better go in the back room.

HERTHA [*turning to the shelves*]: No. I'll be all right.

[*Miss Peabody closes the door and shakes her umbrella and comes briskly up to the desk.*]

MISS PEABODY: I know it's closing time, Birdie, but I've just got to see the new *Vogue*. I bought some of that silk print at Gillam's. They had the most marvelous sale, and—

MISS SCHLAGMANN: The new *Vogue's* out.

MISS PEABODY [*disappointed*]: Oh, is it?

MISS SCHLAGMANN: Yes. Mrs. Critchfield has it. She's using one of those patterns, too.

MISS PEABODY: Oh. Something for Heavenly, I guess. Hmmmm. I guess she's planning to sew on a trousseau this spring.

MISS SCHLAGMANN: Trousseau?

MISS PEABODY: Yes. Haven't you heard? [*Glances sharply at Hertha's back.*] I hope I'm not letting the cat out of the bag. That Arthur Shannon created such an excitement when he came back to town— I'm afraid there'll be quite a few disappointed young

ladies when they make the announcement! [*She giggles shrilly.*]
Did you ever see such a rain? Forty-eight hours without a let up.
But that's April for you. OHH! I have a run in my stocking!
Hello, Hertha.

HERTHA [*barely turning*]: Good evening.

MISS PEABODY [*simpering*]: You were so quiet I didn't know you
were there. I've got to be running. I'm going to Memphis tomorrow. Did you see the *Commercial-Appeal*? Fifty percent reduction
on furs at Hess and Williamson! Isn't that marvelous? That's
where I got the muskrat cape I'm wearing with my brown tweed
suit. Oh, heavens it's nearly nine! You'll save the new *Vogue* for
me? —Good night!

MISS SCHLAGMANN: Good night.

MISS PEABODY [*with marvelous gaiety*]: Good night, Hertha!

[*She laughs and snatches up her umbrella and darts out the
door. All of her actions have that brilliant, exaggerated animation which is characteristic of some southern spinsters. Miss
Schlagmann glances uneasily at Hertha's back. Hertha slowly
raises another book and places it on the shelf. As she does so the
clock strikes nine in a slow, gentle tone.*]

MISS SCHLAGMANN: We're half an hour late. Hertha, you go on
home, you don't need to wait for me.

HERTHA [*turning slowly*]: No. I'll wait till you're ready.

MISS SCHLAGMANN: All right! We'll stop in Greenbaum's and
have a hot chocolate! It will help you sleep.

HERTHA [*dully*]: Yes.

[*Miss Schlagmann retires to the back room and closes the door. Hertha sits down mechanically at the desk and stares in front of her. Her face has a dead expressionless look. After a moment, the outer door is pushed open and Arthur enters—he is drunk, disheveled, his flannel coat and trousers bedraggled with rain and his hair hanging over his forehead. He leans against the door and grins satirically at Hertha.*]

ARTHUR: Good evening, Miss Neilson!

HERTHA: Arthur! [*She touches her hair.*] I wasn't expecting you. You didn't call last night. [*She notices his strange appearance.*] Arthur, what's wrong with you, Arthur?

ARTHUR [*laughing*]: Excuse my experience! —I've come here to show you that southern chivalry is still in flower.

HERTHA: I'm afraid you've been drinking.

ARTHUR: She's afraid I've been drinking. —You put it so tactfully, Miss Neilson. Yes, I'm drunk. You ought to try it sometime yourself. It's exciting. Makes everything look different. Even you, Miss Neilson, you look almost human tonight!

HERTHA: What have you done this for? Arthur, why have you gotten yourself in such a condition?

ARTHUR: Haven't you ever seen a drunk man before? Sure you have. Your father, the Terrible Swede, as they call him. He comes home polluted on Saturday nights, so I hear. Makes a big scene, throws things, calls you names. So what are you getting so puritanical for?

HERTHA [*stiffening*]: Is that amusing to you? Are you laughing because of that?

ARTHUR [*a bit ashamed*]: Sure. Everything's funny tonight. [*He rubs his forehead confusedly.*] Excuse me. Heavenly gave me some liquor and told me to go out and get drunk—so I did.

HERTHA: Heavenly Critchfield—?

ARTHUR: Yes. I told her that I was in love with her, and she said that I should go out and get drunk because that was the only thing that would do me any good. So I got drunk. It's the first time I ever got drunk in my life and it was swell. Till I started thinking about her again making love to Dick Miles.

HERTHA: Arthur! I'm sorry, I— [*She extends her hand towards him in a slight, pitying gesture.*]

ARTHUR: I can forget all that with you, can't I? You're a girl, too. You could make love as well as she could. But not with Dick Miles. With me. [*He moves toward her. Hertha steps back.*] What are you backing away for? Are you scared? That's flattering. Nobody's ever been scared of me before. I was like you, Hertha. I hid behind books all the time because they used to call me a sissy when I was a kid in school. I never got over that. Not till tonight when I got drunk. God! I never knew it could be so good to get drunk and feel like a man inside. Literature and the arts. Stravinsky, Beethoven, Brahms. Concerts, matinees, recitals— what's all that? If I told you you'd blush. You don't like that kind of language. Sure, I sat through all of that stuff and thought it was great. Got my stuff published in those little magazines with the big cultural movements. Art for art's sake. Give America back to the Indians. I thought I was being highbrow. Intellectual. The hell with that stuff. Dick Miles's got the right idea. He was the one that she gave herself to, not me, not me. The one that got drunk and had himself a good time, he was the one that got Heavenly, and me with my intellectual pretensions, my fancy education, and my father's money—what did I get? Pushed in the face! Thrown over for a boy that clerks in a drugstore because he knows how to make love and I don't! Well now I can, too. I can get drunk and act like the rest of them. How about it, Miss Neilson? Why don't you come out from behind those tortoise-shell glasses of yours? [*He reaches across the table and plucks them off.*]

HERTHA: Arthur, please go home. [*She crosses in front of the desk.*] Don't touch me!

ARTHUR [*laughing*]: Don't touch you? Yes. That's it—purity! The Carnegie Vestal! [*He crosses toward her.*]

HERTHA: No! Don't touch me!

ARTHUR: Why not? It would do you some good. You with your books, your anthologies, your metaphysical poets. William Blake and John Donne. They're dead, Hertha. All your lovers are dead and bound up in books. They can't touch you. They can't make love to you tonight. They've been in the ground too long. Don't you know that? [*He turns out the suspended light above.*] This is life and you're scared of it. You've never come up against it before. You haven't found it in any of your alphabetical files. It's taken you by surprise, Hertha, the way it took me when I came back from Europe and saw Heavenly Critchfield again, laughing at me the way that she used to. It hurts you. It's big and awful and crazy and makes you want to run and hide from it. But you can't, Hertha. Hiding doesn't do any good. [*He catches one of her hands which she holds before her in a defensive gesture.*] You've got little hands—they're little candle-wax hands.

HERTHA [*faintly*]: Let go of me, Arthur.

ARTHUR: No. I won't let go.

HERTHA: Please do.

ARTHUR: No.

HERTHA: If you don't I'll have to call Miss Schlagmann.

ARTHUR: Go ahead. Call her. —Haven't you ever been kissed? No. Only in books. By William Blake and John Donne. "Go, and catch a falling star, /Get with child a mandrake root." —Those are your lovers but they've got cold lips. They've been in the ground so long not even April can make them warm, again, Hertha. But I'm not cold. Heavenly thinks I am but she's mistaken. The whiskey's made me warm for a change. I'm hot inside. If I touched you with my lips you'd think you'd been scorched by fire. You'd crumple up like a little white moth that's flown into the candle flame, Hertha. That's what you'd do. [*He pulls her against him.*]

HERTHA [*breathlessly*]: No, no, please let me go.

[*He kisses her. She struggles and then is limp in his arms. After a moment he thrusts her away from him. There is a long pause. The stunned expression recedes from her face and she moves a step toward him.*]

You kissed me, Arthur. [*She touches her lips wonderingly.*]

ARTHUR [*hoarsely*]: Excuse me. I was drunk. [*He averts his face in distaste.*]

HERTHA: You kissed me. —It isn't Heavenly Critchfield you're in love with, it's me! Isn't it, Arthur? It's me! [*She smiles raptly like a child.*]

[*Arthur is shocked out of his drunkenness and repelled by his own action and by Hertha's unexpected reaction to it.*]

ARTHUR [*in confusion*]: I didn't know what I was doing. I'm sorry. [*He goes back a few steps.*] I'd better be going.

HERTHA [*blind with inner brightness*]: Arthur! Now I can tell you! —I love you! I love you. So much that I've nearly gone mad! Oh, God, why didn't you know, why didn't you know? [*Slowly she extends her hand toward the shaded light on the table.*] Arthur! Take me out of here, Arthur, some place where we can be together. [*She turns the light off.*]

ARTHUR [*moving away from her*]: No, I don't want you Hertha.

HERTHA: Arthur!

ARTHUR: Don't you understand? I don't want you! [*Pause.*] I didn't know you were like that. I thought you were different.

HERTHA [*agonized*]: Arthur!

ARTHUR: You— you *disgust* me!

[*His shadow can be seen moving uncertainly toward the door —it closes and he is gone. A wild cry breaks from Hertha's lips and she falls to her knees. After a moment Miss Schlagmann comes out of the stacks, running.*]

MISS SCHLAGMANN: Hertha! What's happened, child? [*She turns the light on.*]

HERTHA [*vaguely*]: There was a man. He scared me. I fainted — please get me some water.

MISS SCHLAGMANN: Hertha! I'll call the police!

HERTHA: No, no! Nothing happened! [*She sobs like a child.*] I want to go home, I want to go home!

MISS SCHLAGMANN: Hertha, poor Hertha! — I'll get you a glass of water!

[*She rushes into the other room. With a choked cry Hertha darts out the front door. When Miss Schlagmann returns with the glass of water, she has disappeared.*]

Hertha! Where are you child? Good heavens, she's gone!

[*Miss Schlagmann rushes out the front door and can be heard calling Hertha's name several times. She returns, frustrated— still holding glass of water. She continues, vaguely.*]

She's gone. . . .

[*She looks helplessly at the glass of water and then slowly, mechanically, pours it into the bowl of yellow jonquils on the desk—*]

SLOW CURTAIN

It is the next evening in the Critchfield living room. Aunt Lila is sewing in her rocker. Heavenly enters slowly in a white cellophane rain cape.

LILA: Still raining?

HEAVENLY [*looking stunned*]: Oh. Yes.

LILA: What's the matter with you?

HEAVENLY: He's gone.

LILA: Richard?

HEAVENLY: Yes.

LILA: Left town, you mean?

HEAVENLY: Yes. —I don't want to talk about it.

LILA: Don't be so tragic. Sit down here and let's get this thing straightened out.

HEAVENLY: Some things can't be straightened out, Auntie.

LILA: I've never known anything yet didn't straighten itself out if you gave it time enough.

HEAVENLY: Time! Yes! A couple of centuries—

LILA: That's how it looks when you're young.

HEAVENLY [*suddenly angry*]: You don't know how it feels!

LILA: Yes, I do know! And I know it's hard to be young! Almost as hard as it is to be old! Sometimes it's even harder because when you're old—you get so you appreciate a good cup of coffee! But the young ones, the kids like you, they think the sun won't rise tomorrow unless they get what they want.

HEAVENLY [*coming down a bit from her anger and despair*]: Have you got a cigarette?

LILA [*brightly*]: A whole pack of 'em. My dividend came in from the compress stock!

HEAVENLY: Thanks.

LILA: By the way, I'm making you a new dress out of some goods I bought at Power's.

HEAVENLY: Thanks, Auntie.

LILA: It's got a lot of red in it. Your mother thinks it's tacky. But I always say that spring's a damn good excuse for wearing bright colors.

HEAVENLY: It's no use, Auntie. I don't feel like being bucked up. [*Her voice catches.*]

LILA: That's right. Go on and do a little crying—and then go upstairs and get dressed for your dinner date.

HEAVENLY [*sobbing.*]: Do you think I'm going out?

LILA: Of course you are. You aren't the sort of girl that gives up going to parties. I was, and look where it got me. [*She offers*

Heavenly a light.] Here. Smoke your cigarette. Cigarettes were made for moments like these. Girls didn't smoke 'em back in the days when I had my big romantic catastrophes. I used to go out in the hayloft and stuff my mouth full of straw which wasn't nearly so nice. They had rats in the hayloft. I remember once when I was right on the point of deciding to kill myself when one of those big gray monsters trotted over my ankle and gave me such a fit of the shudders that I completely forgot about my broken heart.

HEAVENLY [*rising impatiently*]: Oh, I haven't got any broken heart.

LILA: No. They're out of style. Where's he gone to?

HEAVENLY: To work on the levee. That was his big ambition, that's what he wanted to do. He said it took a flannel shirt and pair of boots to make him feel like a man. —He wanted me to go with him. Me! Live like a nigger on a lousy river barge. He expected me to do that.

LILA: Doesn't he give you credit for having a lick of sense?

HEAVENLY: Oh, I don't know. I might do it if he hadn't been so casual about it. He didn't call me all day so I went down to the drugstore, and the soda jerk told me he'd quit his job and gone to Friar's Point and left a note for me in an empty Alka-Seltzer bottle.

LILA: Huh! What did the note say?

HEAVENLY: If I wanted him, I could meet him in Friar's Point tonight. And get married.

LILA: You wouldn't do a fool thing like that.

HEAVENLY: I don't know.

LILA: He's the restless kind. He's never stuck at anything very long.

HEAVENLY: No, he goes from one thing to another.

LILA: One of these drifters.

HEAVENLY: It isn't just that. He isn't satisfied with the things that other people are satisfied with.

LILA: No. You can't blame him for that. But that isn't a very good reason for marrying him. He wanted to get away from the drugstore and the town. Maybe he'd be wanting to get away from you next.

HEAVENLY: I know. I can't be sure.

LILA: You could never be sure.

HEAVENLY: If I thought I could hold him I'd take a chance on the rest. I'd live like a nigger for him on a lousy river barge. I'd even do that, if I thought he wouldn't decide in the end that I was just another thing that he wanted to break away from.

LILA: When they've got the itch in them shoes there's nothing but six feet of dirt can ever make 'em stay put.

HEAVENLY: Tell me what to do.

LILA: You've got a date with Arthur Shannon tonight. Go upstairs and get dressed for it.

HEAVENLY: No!

LILA: I know that sounds like an awful anticlimax to a broken heart or whatever you call it nowadays, but so was the rat that ran over my ankle in the hayloft, and it was the rat that brought me back to my senses and made me see what a sentimental fool I was being! You're better off than I was. You've got another to fall back on.

HEAVENLY: Arthur? I don't think I could ever care much for him.

LILA: Why not?

HEAVENLY: He doesn't seem quite human. All he does is talk and talk.

LILA: He'll get over that.

HEAVENLY: Oh, God, I don't know what to do!

VOICE OF MESSENGER BOY: Cutrere's!

MRS. CRITCHFIELD: Flowers? How lovely! [*She enters with an open box.*] Look at this! Just look! It's talisman roses! Heavenly! Arthur's sent you a corsage! To wear to the Country Club tonight.

HEAVENLY: Oh, I know, I know.

MRS. CRITCHFIELD [*turning to Lila*]: What's the matter with her? What's she crying about?

LILA: Richard Miles left town.

MRS. CRITCHFIELD: Well. Good riddance! I told you how much you could depend on a boy of that kind. —[*She decides to take no further notice of Heavenly's grief.*] Look at this! Did you ever see anything more exquisite? [*She holds the corsage up to Heavenly's shoulder.*] It's going to look lovely on your blue knitted suit.

HEAVENLY [*pushing the corsage aside*]: Let go of me! Leave me alone!

MRS. CRITCHFIELD: Well, that's gratitude for you!

LILA: Leave her alone, Esmeralda.

MRS. CRITCHFIELD: Oh, I know that you were fond of him, Heavenly, but I can't help feeling that his leaving town's the most fortunate thing that *could* have happened.

HEAVENLY: Fond of him. [*She laughs wildly.*] I was crazy about him. You ought to know that.

MRS. CRITCHFIELD: I won't hear anymore about that disgusting business.

HEAVENLY [*practically shouting*]: Crazy about him, do you hear?

MRS. CRITCHFIELD: That horrible—

LILA: Esmeralda!

HEAVENLY: Do you think I'm going to give him up?

MRS. CRITCHFIELD: Of course you're going to give him up. You're going to forget all about him.

HEAVENLY: I won't!

MRS. CRITCHFIELD: You're going to be sensible now.

HEAVENLY: That's what you think!

MRS. CRITCHFIELD: You're going upstairs and get dressed!

HEAVENLY: I'm going upstairs and pack my grip!

MRS. CRITCHFIELD: Do what?

HEAVENLY: I'm going to Friar's Point. Dick's going to meet me there. We're going to get married!

MRS. CRITCHFIELD [aghast]: No!

HEAVENLY: Yes. By a colored preacher. And we're going to live on a river barge.

MRS. CRITCHFIELD: You wouldn't dare—!

HEAVENLY: I thought you'd know by now how much I'd dare to do. Didn't I open your eyes when I told you what had been going on between him and me? Yes, an affair! The gossips were right this time, you can chalk it up in their favor. But I'm not as immoral as you are, I'm not as indecent as you want to make me. I'm not going to give myself to one man and then go marry another that I don't even like. No, hell, no! I'm gonna take the nine o'clock train to Friar's Point and marry Dick and you can't stop me! [She flies out of the room.]

MRS. CRITCHFIELD [she is nearly prostrate]: Oh! Call her father!

LILA: No. Leave this to me, Esmeralda.

MRS. CRITCHFIELD: Get Oliver this instant! We've got to stop her!

LILA: Now don't go all to pieces. Is it true what she said about her and the boy having had an affair?

MRS. CRITCHFIELD [choked]: Yes, it's true.

LILA: When did she tell you?

MRS. CRITCHFIELD: Don't stand there and ask me questions!

LILA: If it's true then maybe she'd better go and marry the boy.

MRS. CRITCHFIELD: No! I'd never permit it! She can marry Arthur Shannon.

LILA: Does he know about her and Richard?

MRS. CRITCHFIELD: No, of course he doesn't. Do you think we want it published in all the papers?

LILA: Why didn't you get Oliver to go and see the boy and get it straightened out?

MRS. CRITCHFIELD: Oliver would have shot him! Wouldn't that have created a nice scandal!

LILA: Oliver wouldn't have done any such thing.

MRS. CRITCHFIELD: Then you don't think family honor means anything to your brother?

LILA: Family honor hasn't got anything to do with normal young people's emotions.

MRS. CRITCHFIELD: Normal! Emotions. It's easy to see what side of the family she gets her indecency from.

LILA: Indecency nothing! She's human that's all. Maybe a little too human. And if she gets that from the Critchfields I'm not ashamed of it.

MRS. CRITCHFIELD: No! You're all shameless.

LILA: Maybe so, but that's beside the point. Did Heavenly tell you anything else?

MRS. CRITCHFIELD: No. There haven't been any serious consequences.

LILA: Well, I'm going upstairs.

MRS. CRITCHFIELD [*desperately hopeful*]: You're going to talk her out of it?

LILA: I'm not going to talk her in or out of anything. I'm going to help her decide for herself.

MRS. CRITCHFIELD: Lila!

LILA: It's the only thing to do.

MRS. CRITCHFIELD: I understand your attitude. You're doing this because you hate the Shannons.

LILA: I don't hate the Shannons. [*She goes out.*]

MRS. CRITCHFIELD [*shouting after her*]: Yes, you do. You're holding a grudge! [*The doorbell rings.*] Oh, that's Arthur.

[*She pulls herself desperately together and scurries about the shabby room putting things straight. Her actions show a pathetic inability to rise above trivialities, even in a time of crisis. She switches on the light above Colonel Wayne's portrait; then she rushes into the hall and can be heard admitting Arthur in her best social manner. She ushers him into the living room talking a mile a minute to cover up her nervousness. This should be played for comedy but not farce.*]

133

Oh, my dear boy, it's started raining again! Your lovely white panama hat, did it get very damp? [*She enters the room followed by Arthur whose manner is very constrained.*] Oh, I think it was such a dreadful shame about last night. Susan Lamphrey'd been planning that lawn party for weeks and then the rains came along and spoiled all the nice preparations. But that's April for you! I suppose they just had to move everything indoors. Fortunately they have a very spacious downstairs—

ARTHUR [*politely disinterested*]: Oh, they have.

MRS. CRITCHFIELD: Yes, that's the mahvelous thing about those old ante-bellum houses, they knew absolutely *nothing* about the economy of space. It's awfully hard to keep them warm in winter but in spring and summer I think they're simply delightful.

ARTHUR: Yes. Yes, I suppose so.

MRS. CRITCHFIELD: Oh, I often wish we hadn't given up the old Wayne plantation. The house was nearly two hundred years old. It was the most historic place in the Delta. That's Colonel Wayne's picture there on the wall.

ARTHUR: Oh, is it?

MRS. CRITCHFIELD: Yes. He led the charge up Cemetery Hill. If we'd won the war he would've been president of the Confederacy. He was a great friend of Jefferson Davis. Upstairs we have the very bed that Mr. Davis slept in when he visited our plantation. It's in Heavenly's room.

ARTHUR: Oh, is it?

MRS. CRITCHFIELD: Yes, that chair is hers, too. Mr. Critchfield's always nagging me to have things upholstered, but you know I just can't bear to change them when they're so rich in tradition and all. Sometime I'm going to have you look through our family papers, Arthur. Writers are always so interested in things like that. With your literary gifts I'm quite sure you could write some things up for me. For instance that very dramatic little episode that took place on Colonel Wayne's plantation the second year of the war when it was rumored that Sherman had crossed the border—

[*A loud crash is heard upstairs.*]

Oh, heavens, what's that? [*She pauses nervously, recovers and smiles.*] Heavenly must be romping with the dog! What were we talking about? Oh, yes of course, books! I have a cousin who writes them. Had one published. I forget just what the name of it was. [*Another loud noise is heard above.*] Oh, yes, *The Stroke of Doom*, that was it! A mystery novel based on the most remarkable coincidence that actually took place. [*The noise continues.*] Seems to me the setting was somewhere in Europe. Or was it Africa? Oh, no, it was Australia! And just think, Cousin Alfred was an invalid—he'd never been out of Mississippi in all his life! He got his information, every bit of it, out of the *Encyclopedia Britannica*.

Heavenly's voice [*upstairs*]: I won't, I tell you, I won't.

[*A door slams violently.*]

MRS. CRITCHFIELD [*in extreme agitation*]: Perhaps I'd better go up and tell Heavenly that you're here— If you'll excuse me for just a moment.

ARTHUR [*rising*]: Certainly, Mrs. Critchfield.

[*Mrs. Critchfield rushes out. Arthur looks keenly distressed and puzzled. After a brief interval Aunt Lila enters.*]

LILA: Good evening, young man.

ARTHUR: Oh, good evening, Miss Critchfield.

[*Lila adjusts her glasses and looks at him sharply; she touches her forehead with a handkerchief.*]

LILA: Eau de cologne—it's very refreshing when you've been through a nervous ordeal! [*She smiles.*] I've been trying to talk some sense into my niece's head. You probably wondered about that racket up there. Sit down and I'll tell you.

ARTHUR: Uh—thanks.

LILA: I haven't had much chance to get acquainted with Gale Shannon's boy. Tell me about yourself. What are you going to do, what are you planning to be? A young nincompoop all your life? [*She laughs kindly.*] No, you look too much like your father for that. I used to go out with Gale Shannon when I was a girl. He threw me over for your mother, God bless him, but he's still aces with me. [*Then she continues quite seriously and gently.*] Are you in love with Heavenly?

ARTHUR [*rising gravely*]: Yes, Ma'am. I do have that misfortune.

LILA: Misfortune? I wouldn't say that!

ARTHUR: Neither would I, Ma'am, if I thought I had a chance in the world.

LILA: I think you have got a chance if you take it. But it's absolutely your last.

ARTHUR: Yes, Ma'am? What's that?

LILA: She's planning to run off with a young jackanapes that's gone to work on the river.

136

ARTHUR: Richard Miles?

LILA: Yes. There's nothing wrong with that boy and there's nothing wrong with Heavenly, but the two of 'em can't team together, they'd never run the same way— So if you're sure you love her and you want her there's just one thing for you to do.

ARTHUR: What's that?

LILA: Grab her and don't let her go!

ARTHUR: Grab her?

LILA: Certainly. The main reason Nature's provided you with arms, is so you can grab what you want, and by the Eternal, young man, if you don't grab things in this world you don't have a coon's chance of ever getting 'em. Do you think a drink would do you any good?

ARTHUR: Yes, Ma'am, I think it might.

LILA [*producing a bottle from the bookcase*]: Take a swig of this. It's Oliver's.

ARTHUR [*taking the bottle*]: That's funny.

LILA: What?

ARTHUR: Nothing much. Just a little coincidence.

LILA: Take a good one. She'll be flying down those steps in a minute—pretendin' like she's going to the Country Club. But she isn't. I know what she's got up her sleeve. She's going to ask you to drive her over to Friar's Point where that boy's gone. Don't do it. Just grab her and make her stay here. And make her like it. Heavenly's no angel, in fact she's a regular little hussy. I think she likes you better'n you think if you treat her like she needs to be treated— Here she's coming! Let me get out of here quick!

[*Aunt Lila flies out the rear door as Heavenly enters. Her eyes have a hectic brilliance. She is like some beautiful wild animal at the point of flight.*]

ARTHUR [*starting forward*]: Heavenly—

HEAVENLY : What?

ARTHUR: I thought you weren't going to the Country Club.

HEAVENLY : How did you know? Did Auntie tell you?

ARTHUR [*tensely*]: I thought you were going to Friar's Point—

HEAVENLY: Shhh! Mother doesn't know. So be quiet till we get outside. [*She crosses to him.*] I want you to do me a big favor, Arthur. I want you to drive me over to Friar's Point tonight— Will you?

ARTHUR: Heavenly, I— Heavenly. [*He suddenly grabs her in his arms.*]

HEAVENLY [*struggling*]: What do you think you're doing?

[*Arthur kisses her wildly. She struggles to free herself, strikes at him with her fists, but he doesn't release her.*]

Stop, Arthur. You're hurting me! Don't!

[*He slightly relaxes his grip. She continues aghast.*]

You must be out of your senses, Arthur Shannon!

ARTHUR: Yes, I'm crazy. [*He kisses her again.*]

HEAVENLY: Don't Arthur. I won't stand for this!

ARTHUR: You won't?

HEAVENLY: No, I *won't*.

[*Arthur kisses her repeatedly: on the lips, throat, shoulders. Heavenly gasps for breath, stops resisting. She leans passively against him. There is a long pause.*]

ARTHUR [*in a soft anxious voice*]: Heavenly, have I—hurt you, Heavenly?

HEAVENLY: No, I— I guess it doesn't matter. [*She smiles slightly.*] I really didn't think you were capable of doing anything like this.

ARTHUR: I didn't mean to do it. I was—out of my senses. [*He starts to release her.*]

HEAVENLY: No, don't let go of me. Don't let me go.

ARTHUR: You don't want me to?

HEAVENLY: No. I want to rest like this for awhile. I'm so tired. I was going to do something crazy Arthur. Going someplace where I wasn't wanted. But now I guess I don't have to. Maybe this is the answer.

ARTHUR: Heavenly, what do you mean?

HEAVENLY: I don't know yet. Give me a cigarette, please. [*He does.*] Thanks. I'll take a few drags and then I'll be able to tell you.

[*She sinks on the sofa and leans back.*]

ARTHUR: I'm sorry, Heavenly. I can't tell you how I despise myself.

HEAVENLY: Sorry, for what?

ARTHUR: For acting like an animal.

HEAVENLY: Needn't be sorry for that. That's the first thing you've done to convince me that you're a human being. I didn't think you were alive till just now. I thought you were just a sort of walking dictionary or something. I didn't think you could use your lips for anything but putting long words together. And now—well, I'm glad to find out that I was mistaken!

ARTHUR: What were you going to Friar's Point for?

HEAVENLY: I was going to marry Dick. He's gone there. We've been in love for a long time, ever since sophomore cotillion at high school about seven years ago. And you can't expect people to go on loving each other all that time without something happenin' between them.

ARTHUR: You don't need to—

HEAVENLY: Repeat the horrible confession? That's what mother called it. I told her the other day about Dick and me, but she was still anxious for me to give him up and take you. She approves of you, Arthur, and she thinks dishonesty's the best policy in love affairs— She didn't want me to tell you the awful truth.

ARTHUR: I'm glad that you did.

HEAVENLY: Why? Does it make it easier for you to forget me?

ARTHUR: No. I'd never try to do that.

HEAVENLY: Then do you still want me? Even secondhand?

ARTHUR: Yes. Anyway I can have you.

HEAVENLY: All right. [*She puts out her cigarette.*] It's all settled. Instead of marrying Dick and living on a lousy river barge, I'm going to marry Arthur Shannon and live in the biggest house in town!

ARTHUR: Heavenly, is that how you feel about it?

HEAVENLY [*gently*]: No, not really—if you hadn't made love to me I would have gone to Friar's Point.

ARTHUR: But you aren't going now?

HEAVENLY: No, I'm not going now. Can you reach the light? [*He extinguishes the table lamp.*] Thanks. It's so much nicer in the dark, especially when there's rain and lightnin' outside. [*He sits beside her.*] What kind of talcum powder do you use? I like the smell of it. [*She leans on his shoulder.*] Mmmm. I like your flannel coat sleeve too. It feels nice. It's astonishing how many nice thing I've found out about you, Arthur Shannon, in the last few minutes. —For God's sake, don't start talking! —When you're making love to a girl you should always be quiet because there aren't any words that are good enough to say what you mean anyhow. . .

[*The phone rings in the hall. Heavenly continues, a slight catch in her voice.*]

That's Dick calling from Friar's Point to find out whether or not I'm coming.

ARTHUR: Don't get up. Don't answer it.

HEAVENLY: Why not?

ARTHUR: Because if you do you'll never come back.

HEAVENLY: All right. I'll stay here with you. I won't move.

[*Aunt Lila can be heard answering the phone in the hall. Her voice comes indistinctly through the closed door. After a few moments she opens it and stands in the doorway. She turns on the light.*]

LILA [*with constraint*]: I beg your pardon.

HEAVENLY [*laughing*]: Auntie, don't be so formal. You know I've been kissed before.

LILA: I wasn't thinking of that.

HEAVENLY: Oh. What were you thinking of?

LILA: Someone just called.

HEAVENLY: For me?

LILA: No.

HEAVENLY [*sharply*]: Don't be so mysterious, Auntie! What's happened?

[*Lila turns slowly to Arthur.*]

LILA: Arthur. You haven't heard about Hertha Neilson?

ARTHUR [*anxiously*]: Heard *what* about her?

LILA [*after a slight pause*]: She was killed last night. They found her body in the freight yards.

[*Arthur is stunned.*]

HEAVENLY: The freight yards!

LILA: Yes. It wasn't identified till an hour ago.

HEAVENLY [*looking at Arthur*]: Auntie, why did you have to come in here and tell him like this?

LILA: Because that isn't all. Miss Schlagmann told me that Hertha Neilson and a young man had a violent scene of some kind in the library before it happened.

HEAVENLY: What young man? What did Miss Schlagmann say what man it was?

LILA: She didn't see him and Hertha Neilson didn't say. But maybe Arthur could tell you.

HEAVENLY: No. Leave Arthur alone. Whatever happened I'm sure it wasn't his fault.

LILA: Maybe not. But I think he ought to be prepared for what people are likely to say.

HEAVENLY: What can they say? Everybody knows the poor girl was out of her mind.

[*Arthur rises slowly and goes blindly across the room toward the French doors. Lightning glimmers through them.*]

Arthur, I know it's dreadful. But it wasn't your fault. [*She turns to Lila.*] Auntie, what are you standing there for? Please get out!

LILA: I think Arthur ought to leave now.

HEAVENLY: No. Why should he?

ARTHUR: She's right. I'll have to go.

HEAVENLY: Please, Auntie! Get out!

[*Lila exits.*]

Tell me, Arthur—was it you?

ARTHUR: Yes.

HEAVENLY: What happened?

ARTHUR: I took your advice, I got drunk. After I left you and your lover at the party, I got drunk, but I didn't go across the Sunflower like you suggested. I went to the library instead.

HEAVENLY: What happened? You'd better tell me.

ARTHUR: Oh, God. I can't. The freight yards.

HEAVENLY: Don't think about that.

ARTHUR [*verging on hysteria*]: I wonder how many boxcars there were last night? Sometimes they're terribly long. Once I counted fifty-seven.

HEAVENLY: Don't, Arthur! Hold on to yourself!

ARTHUR: No wonder she was dead when they found her. Not identified till just now. How did they ever find out? Because she wasn't down at the library this morning? The Storybook Lady— the dark-haired princess in the Magic Tower. And I called her— The Carnegie Vestal—I called her that. And kissed her. And then she came alive in my arms and begged me to take her. Because she was like I was, lonely and hungry, and I—I lost my desire. I told her that she was disgusting—

HEAVENLY: You didn't do that!

ARTHUR: Yes.

HEAVENLY: That was cruel.

ARTHUR: Yes. And after that she screamed. And I ran out the door and all I could hear for blocks and blocks was that screaming. And then it was quiet. Nothing but rain on my face. I was glad that I'd gotten away. And then a funny thing happened. [*He turns slowly toward Heavenly.*] I came to an alley. It was in back of your house. It was filled with the fresh smell of roses. I went sort of crazy. Covered my face with those flowers and whispered your name. [*He turns away.*] And I guess about that time Hertha was standing out in the freight yards with the rain on her face, too—and the engine's light in her eyes, screaming— We were driving that engine last night, Heavenly, you and me.

HEAVENLY: No.

ARTHUR: We were inside those boxcars, we were the ones that killed her.

HEAVENLY: No. Arthur. You couldn't help it that you loved me instead of her.

ARTHUR: Loved you—yes—I told her that. She climbed up the hill and stood between the two dead trees and said she was one of them now. I was too full of myself to know what she meant or to care.

HEAVENLY: That's natural. We're all of us full of ourselves. [*She kisses him.*]

ARTHUR: How can you stand to do that?

HEAVENLY: Because I want to. It's funny how I feel toward you now. So much diff'rent. [*She clings to him.*] You've done me a favor tonight. You've taught me something very important about the nature of love. It's our bodies we love with mostly. When you kissed me just now, I could have believed it was him, Dick— It gave me the same sensation, exactly the same— You've made me love you, Arthur.

ARTHUR: How can you talk about *us* after what's happened?

HEAVENLY: Because I was bo'n twice as old as you are an' you'll never catch up.

[*She goes over to the sofa and switches off the small light above Colonel Wayne's portrait. Her voice is low.*]

Come over here and be quiet.

ARTHUR: No. Your Aunt was right. I've got to leave here.

HEAVENLY: Why should you leave?

ARTHUR: Don't you see why? There'll be an investigation and they'll find things out. I'll be disgraced. I'll have to leave town.

HEAVENLY: You're afraid of people?

ARTHUR: Not so much as I'm afraid of myself. I've committed murder and I can't stay here at the scene of the crime. It would hound me.

HEAVENLY: Then take me away with you. I don't want to stay here either.

ARTHUR: I can't take you with me. I've got to be off by myself for awhile. With strangers, Heavenly. They're—they're a sort of—catharsis. Like cold water on your face and hands. They make you feel clean. Whenever I touched you now it would be like dipping my hands in her blood.

HEAVENLY: Arthur. Don't say that.

ARTHUR: It would. —I'm sorry, Heavenly. I'll come back later if you still want me.

HEAVENLY: No. If you leave me now I'll hate you. I'll never want to see you again.

ARTHUR: Maybe that would be a good thing. [*He moves toward the hall.*]

HEAVENLY [*desperately*]: You're a coward. You're running away.

ARTHUR [*dully*]: Yes. That's a habit of mine.

HEAVENLY: You can't leave me now! [*She follows him to the hall door.*]

ARTHUR: Good-bye, Heavenly.

HEAVENLY [*wildly*]: You can't say that, too! *Arthur!*

[*The door is heard closing. Heavenly is in bewildered agony.*]

Oh—

[*Heavenly wanders back to the middle of the room, her eyes dull and exhausted. After a moment Lila comes quietly in.*]

LILA: He's gone?

HEAVENLY: Yes, They've both gone.

LILA: Are you going to Richard?

HEAVENLY: No, he doesn't want me either. He's got what he wanted. But maybe someday he'll want me again. Or maybe Arthur will. I don't know. I'll have to wait and see.

[*She moves slowly toward the hall.*]

LILA: Where are you going?

[*Heavenly turns in the doorway and stares vacantly into space.*]

HEAVENLY: I'm going out and sit on the front porch till one of them comes back.

CURTAIN

TEXTUAL NOTES

Among the Tennessee Williams (TW) papers gathered into several folders marked *Spring Storm*, deposited at the Harry Ransom Humanities Research Center (HRHRC) in 1963, there are two scripts: one is titled *April is the Cruelest Month* (AITCM); and the other is *Spring Storm* (SS). It ought to be noted that while SS is complete, the earlier text, AITCM, is missing eighteen pages and has two other suggested titles on its first page (*Spring Storm* and *Time of Roses*). The rest of the material is fragments: a single page or several consecutive pages, occasionally a whole scene. Adopting the language of film editing, these pages might be called the out-takes—which is to say, dialogue and whole scenes either cut from the play or improved and included in another form.

Because the play was never produced and probably never looked at after TW submitted it to MGM for possible film production (see Introduction), the time sequence of the play was never fully justified. To clarify both the play's actions and the steps needed to remedy the inconsistencies, a short chronology of the play's action is in order: using the Lamphrey's Saturday night lawn party (Act Three, Scene One) as a base, three of the four days and nights of *Spring Storm* are relatively easy to trace. If, at the party, the gossips talk about seeing Dick and Heavenly leaving a tourist cabin "at two o'clock this morning," then Arthur's visit that ends with Heavenly's slipping out to meet Dick takes place Friday night (Act Two, Scene Two). The final scene then takes place on Sunday evening. It is the opening scene, the church picnic, that is hard to place. The usual day for a church picnic would have been a Sunday afternoon, but various references make it seem closer in time to the Friday scenes of Act Two.

But while the day of the picnic is primarily a matter of curiosity, there is a real dramaturgic difficulty for anyone who would edit the last scene, whether for production or publication. Essential to the resolution of SS is the arrival of Arthur Shannon at the Critchfield home in this last scene.

For the play's *scene à faire*—the scene that must be played—takes place between Arthur and Heavenly. But in the script of SS, TW brought Arthur to the house for the wrong reason: to take Heavenly to the Lamphrey's party. Obviously, when he cobbled his various rewrites together, he had forgotten that the Lamphrey's lawn party had already taken place two scenes earlier. The solution is quite simple. In the last scene of the play Arthur now comes to take Heavenly to the Country Club for dinner—a Sunday night date that he had eagerly reminded her of when they first crossed paths on the top of the bluff in the first scene. The original script for the final scene had Mrs. Critchfield still working on the organdy dress for the Lamphrey lawn party. This reference has been dropped in favor of the "blue knitted suit," earlier suggested (Act Two, Scene One) by Mrs. Critchfield for wear to the Country Club with Arthur. Each instance where a change has been made to remove inconsistencies of time and sequential action will be noted below.

There happen to be two different first pages for SS that are isolated, nothing following them, and one of them ought to be described, because it provides authorial proof for an essential fact. This page has *Spring Storm* written at the top in caps; and the first paragraph following the title begins with this sentence: "I think I should preface this play with the explanation or apology that my aim was to write a realistic play about ordinary life." Though later TW would pencil out this beginning paragraph with a broad X, a few lines down he wrote: "The present play is simply a realistic study of human relations, its theme the sexual struggle of youth, against the background of a small Mississippi town in which I once lived with my grandfather who was an Episcopal clergyman." This statement declares what almost all of the place-names used in SS prove: that the fictive Port Tyler is closely modeled on the very real Clarksdale, Mississippi, a small town about seventy miles due south of Memphis, Tennessee and at a ten-mile remove from the Mississippi River. Those instances where I have been able to prove a Clarksdale connection will also be noted below.

In the original text, obviously typed by TW himself, there are many typos; these will be corrected silently.

Page 5 – Stage Directions: *A high windy bluff over the Mississippi—called Lover's Leap.*

There are no high bluffs overlooking the Mississippi River in the Clarksdale area. This impression from my brief visit to Clarksdale for a TW Annual Festival in 1998, was confirmed by John Ruskey who runs the boat trips out of the Friars Point/Clarksdale area. The geological formation that inspired TW in the setting of this first act might well have been the Chickasaw Bluff (the three-hundred-foot high Chickasaw Bluff on the east shore that extends from Cairo, Illinois, down to Memphis), for Williams' beloved grandparents had moved to Memphis in 1931 after the Reverend Walter Edwin Dakin had retired from the St. George Church in Clarksdale. In 1935, TW spent most of the summer in Memphis with Gramps and Grand.

According to TW scholar Allean Hale, in the Columbia, Missouri area where TW spent his earliest college years, starting in 1929, there is a rock formation called Lover's Leap, and this may be the source for the use of the name here.

Page 9 – REVEREND HOOKER: Swear not by the inconstant—April! Her moods are various—

This Shakespearean-styled quote is probably TW's takeoff on *Romeo & Juliet's*: "O swear not by the inconstant moon. . . . " The dash after "inconstant" here suggests a pause needed to substitute "April" for "moon."

Page 13 – HEAVENLY: And now I've made you stop watchin' the *rivuh*—haven't I? (Italics added for identification.)

Prior to this, Heavenly has referred to the body of water that flows below them as the "river." Has TW slipped here? Or is Heavenly's move into Dick's style of pronunciation meant to signify a surrender even as she claims a small victory? The use of accents—when, where and why—needs a careful study to determine whether TW's use of accent and drawl is careless and occasional or subtle and significant.

Page 13 – MRS. ASBURY: Oh, Heavenly!

In TW's typed text of SS this line reads, "Oh, Helen!" In AITCM, the Heavenly character is named "Helen." Was Heavenly a later nickname that stuck? And does Mrs. Asbury still think of her by her given name Helen? Or did TW's memory slip? Without the arcane knowledge of the unpublished AITCM, the reader can only see a confusing mistake. Hence the text here has been harmonized to read "Heavenly."

Page 14 – HEAVENLY: *Satuhday's Children?*

Saturday's Children is a 1927 play by Maxwell Anderson depicting a woebegone newly married couple who feel lonely and frightened. When the wife suggests they have a baby to relieve the isolation, the husband responds: "Do you think I want to join a chain gang?"

Page 15 – DICK: What happened in Czechoslovakia at eleven A.M.

The newspapers of 1937 were filled with the details of rancorous strife in the Sudetenland, as Hitler continued to make demands for the liberation of this German-speaking region that belonged to Czechoslovakia. When the Munich Agreement was signed on September 30, 1938, by Neville Chamberlain, Hitler, Mussolini, and Deladier, the Sudetenland was surrendered to Nazi Germany without Czech consent. Shortly thereafter, British Prime Minister Chamberlain made his now infamous declaration: "I have brought peace in our time."

Page 17 – HEAVENLY: You're foolin'!
SUSAN: I hope to fall dead if I am. I nearly did *anow*.

The word italicized, "anow" is difficult and might be the colloquial remains of a dialect word. This passage originates in AITCM, and there the word appears as "anyow." If read there first, without the knowledge of "anow" in SS, "anyow" would certainly be taken for a typo of "anyhow," and corrected accordingly. The Oxford English Dictionary (OED) contains no entry for "anow"—but a number of variant meanings for "enow," and one of them "just now" is confirmed by the context here.

Page 22 – ARTHUR: You won't forget about our dinner Sunday?

The SS typed text reads: "You won't forget about our dinner tomorrow?" However, consistent with Heavenly's original mention of their

Sunday dinner date (p. 18), the word "tomorrow" has been changed to the word "Sunday."

Page 25 – HERTHA: Did he tell you what places you were going?

At first glance this seems an acceptable phrase and has been left as TW wrote it. But in the '96 Octoberfest rehearsals, this sentence seemed syntactically lacking, and actress Diana LaMar who created Hertha felt it presented a mini-sec of confusion. In the reading the line was given as: "Did he tell you what places you were going to?"

Page 35 – MESSENGER BOY: Cutrere's.

Blanche Cutrer was one of the wealthiest women in Clarksdale and lived in the Cutrer mansion that overlooks the Sunflower River. The name Cutrer will show up again in Williams' *Orpheus Descending* as Carol Cutrere, the sexually aggressive, unmarried daughter of a wealthy family.

Page 36 – Stage Directions: *"emblems of the D.A.R. and D.O.C."*

"Daughters of the American Revolution" and "Daughters of the Confederacy." But the latter, D.O.C. is questionable in some quarters. Joyce Fulton, Secretary of the Carnegie Library in Clarksdale, Mississippi, responding in writing to several of my requests for information about Clarksdale and the South, helped to clarify the D.O.C. matter. In a letter she indicated that she spoke with "a patron genealogically knowledgeable" who told her the following: "D.O.C. cannot represent the Daughters of the Confederacy because that organization is the UNITED Daughters of the Confederacy or UDC as it is frequently called. Rather than D.O.C. perhaps the initials should have been and were probably meant to be D.A.C. which is Daughters of American Colonists," which in her words was "a very elite and snobbish group." Ms. Fulton continued with her own take on the matter: "It could have been that Tennessee was in fact referring to the Daughters of the Confederacy because the organization is often referred to by that name and not United Daughters of the Confederacy. I believe that that organization may be more well known than the Daughters of the American Colonists in the South."

Page 37 – LILA: Some goods I got at Power's spring sale.

Power's was a family-owned women's wear clothing store in Clarksdale that closed only in 1997.

Page 37 – MRS. CRITCHFIELD: Your dividend come in from the *compress stock*? (Italics added.)

A compress is a device for turning cotton into bales. Aunt Lila has invested in the processing of cotton, while her brother Oliver works in the more risky and speculative business of selling cotton.

Page 38 – MRS. CRITCHFIELD: All you know is what Agnes Peabody tells you.

There is a confusion of names here in the script of SS with regard to the person who is the source of gossip regarding a newly discovered local pregnancy. For a few lines further down Aunt Lila comments: "You'd think that Birdie was taking mail orders from the stork." This exchange first appears in AITCM where Birdie Schlagmann is the name of the gossip throughout. But with the newly added library scene to SS, Birdie Schlagmann has a stage appearance as a fully rounded and sympathetic character. So TW probably decided to switch the gossip role to Agnes Peabody whose outrageous persona is best suited for it—but in the process, TW failed to fully harmonize the SS text—which we have done for him in favor of Agnes.

Page 39 – LILA: April really is too early for organdy.

An interesting and quietly acrimonious argument develops between Aunt Lila and Mrs. C. regarding the propriety of Heavenly wearing organdy early in late spring to the Lamphrey's lawn party. For organdy is a thin, semi-transparent fabric made of woven cotton, more commonly worn in warmer weather. Joyce Fulton of the Carnegie Library in Clarksdale added her own gloss: "Crepe myrtle trees grow prolifically in the South and traditionally bloom at Easter time so it would make sense that Esmeralda would not wear white until the crepe myrtles bloomed, for Easter has always been the shoe color gauge."

Page 41 – MRS. CRITCHFIELD: And the Miles boy. . . . Didn't even get through high school. . . .

Despite the fact that Dick did graduate from high school (in 1932—see his response to Dr. Hooker in Act One, Page 8), Mrs. Critchfield uses every opportunity to disparage his character. This is either willful misremembering on her part or TW's inattention to detail.

Page 42 – LILA: Agnes Peabody says he's taken a notion to that librarian . . .

Again, the name of the gossip has been changed from Bertie Schlagmann to Agnes Peabody.

Page 44 – ANNOUNCER'S VOICE: . . . . a little poem by Sara Teasdale. . . .

This poem, "I Shall Not Care," by Sara Teasdale (1884-1933) was published in *Rivers to the Sea* (Macmillan, 1920), and is recited here by the Village Rhymester in its two stanza entirety. Teasdale was a St. Louis poet whose suicide "had deeply affected Tom," according to Lyle Leverich (LL) in *Tom, The Unknown Tennessee Williams*.

Page 46 – MRS. CRITCHFIELD: For a girl your age you show remarkably little sense about our account at Mungers.

Did Mungers give Heavenly compassionate credit? Or is Mrs. Critchfield lying on Page 51 when she states that "Our account's been cut off at Mungers"?

Page 47 – HEAVENLY: Yes, I know. Sunday night.

In the midst of Mrs. Critchfield's denigratory remarks to Heavenly about Dick's lack of professional ambition, she suddenly switches her tactical approach by reminding Heavenly: "You have a dinner engagement with Arthur, you know." The sense of the statement is that the dinner engagement is that night. Reinforcing that sense is Arthur's earlier anxious reminder to Heavenly as they pass each other on the hill in the first scene of the play: "You won't forget our dinner tomorrow night?" But because it is necessary to establish a motive for Arthur's arrival in the last scene of the play—see the notes to the last scene that takes place on Sunday where the problems of motive and chronology demand editorial intervention—Heavenly here is made to say, "Sunday night," two words not in TW's text at this point.

This change, as well as the earlier change in Arthur's speech, is necessary to establish the Sunday night date as planned for and the Friday night encounter as more or less accidental (*see note to Page 22*).

Page 49 – MRS. CRITCHFIELD: A girl whose name is listed under five of six different headings in Zella Armstrong's *Notable Families*.

The full title of this six-volume genealogical work, first published between 1915 and 1933, is actually *Notable Southern Families*. Familiarity has caused Mrs. Critchfield to drop "Southern" from the title, for in her mind notable families could have come from no other place.

Page 56 – OLIVER: Off two points on the Memphis curb. One at New Orleans.

1937 was a disastrous year for cotton, and Oliver Critchfield's terse announcement of falling prices on two spot markets serves to remind that the problem of cotton—once upon a time the white gold of the South—was only getting worse. The past December (1936), cotton had fallen to nine cents a pound, equal to the lows of 1933. Bumper crops had created oversupply and the downward spiral of prices.

Page 57 – MRS. CRITCHFIELD: Ozzie, be careful.

Ozzie was the name of the Williams' family maid who was also a nanny to both young Rose and Tom for the first five or six years of their lives. Ozzie was greatly beloved by both children, and LL believes that her ghost stories at bedtime had a profound influence on TW. In 1916, when young Tom was but five years old, "in a fit of fury he called Ozzie 'a big black nigger.'" (LL, p. 43). Shortly after that Ozzie left and never returned. (For a full description of Ozzie's mysterious departure, see pages 19 and 25-6 in Edwina Dakin Williams' memoir. *Remember Me To Tom* as well as the relevant pages in LL's *Tom*, Chapter 2.)

Page 57 – MRS. CRITCHFIELD: She broke another piece of the Havilland.

Havilland is a valued porcelain first made in Limoges in 1797.

Page 61 – HEAVENLY: How did you know that talisman roses are my favorite flowers?

This flower is mentioned in many catalogues dealing with southern horticulture. "Talisman Roses" is also the title of an unpublished one-act play by TW at the HRHRC, dealing with the same themes as SS.

Page 61 – HEAVENLY: I hate orchids. . . . I've seen 'em at debuts in Memphis and the girls that wear 'em are always those *money-snobs* who give you a look that peels the gilt right off your slippers. (Italics added.)

Money-snobs: Signs of increasing tension between the New South, a money-rich class of manufacturers exploiting non-unionized labor, and the Old South, rich in family lore but land poor. The Critchfields, sometime before the play starts, had taken the first step down toward impoverishment when they sold their land and were left with only storied antiques, such as the bed Jefferson Davis slept in.

Pages 62-63 – HEAVENLY: You'll have a Coke with me, won't you? It's a new kind of drink.

      ARTHUR: I never touch stimulants after six-thirty, especially when I am not sleeping well.

When Coca-Cola first went on the market in 1886—not quite as new drink as Heavenly suggests—there were rumors that it contained cocaine; for it was first promoted as a kind of snake-oil with medicinal properties that could cure headaches. According to Allen Frederick's fact-crammed book, *Secret Formula: How Brilliant Marketing. . . . Made Coca-Cola the Best Known Product in the World*, there was some truth to the cocaine rumor. As early as 1891, when Coca-Cola was analyzed by the Georgia Pharmaceutical Organization, a miniscule amount of cocaine was discovered—so little that it would take the consumption of thirty consecutive bottles of Coca-Cola to produce a cocaine high. Of course, then and now, Coca-Cola contains caffeine, an addictive stimulant.

Page 66 – HEAVENLY: He smells like dead *rose leaves*. (Italics added.)

Rose blossoms don't have leaves—but the OED attests to the phrase "rose-leaves" as a substitute for rose "petals"; and this usage goes all

the way back to Chaucer. If TW didn't know this phrase from colloquial usage, he probably knew it from Shelley's 1821 poem, "To ——
[Music, When Soft Voices Die]" the fifth and sixth lines of which
read: "Rose leaves, when the rose is dead,/ Are heaped for the
beloved's bed."

Page 68 – ARTHUR: It's an autographed first edition of Humphrey
Hardcastle.

The poet Humphrey Hardcastle seems to be TW's satiric creation.

Page 78 – Stage Directions: *It is later that night.*

This scene was *not* a part of the only surviving complete typed text
of SS; nor is there anything resembling it in AITCM. I found two
drafts of this scene among the many discarded pages that belong to
the out-take pile. When first encountered, I was moved by the ten-
derness and calm that prevails in this late night meeting—something
akin to reflective mood music, and in sharp contrast to the intense
contentiousness that begins with the first scene and never lessens. It
serves as a caesura that permits one to relax and breathe deeply, the
right kind of preparation for an intermission.

  The scene accomplishes several things, but affects the plot and
outcome not at all. Oliver C. is never given his own space in this
play; a time without Esmeralda picking away at him. Here he is able
to open up and answer Heavenly's plaintive question in such a way
that the title is layered with deeper meaning.

Page 78 – MR. CRITCHFIELD: What are you doing down here at *three
o'clock* in the morning? (Italics added.)

The text had "two in the morning"—but that has been emended to
"three" to permit a reasonable time-flow for sequential action. For
in the scene that follows, Heavenly is reported to have left Moon
Lake Casino at two A.M. on the same evening as this late night meeting with her father. With the change here to three A.M., Heavenly is
allowed an hour to get herself together and arrive home.

Page 82 – Stage Directions: *The scene is the Lamphrey's lawn party. . . .
Japanese lanterns are strung overhead.*

The Cutrer mansion in Clarksdale was famous for its use of Japanese lanterns for its evening parties that spread across the spacious grounds on a small bluff overlooking the Sunflower River. This mansion, modeled after an Italian villa, was built in 1916 by Blanche Clark Cutrer (daughter of Clarksdale founder John Clark), and her husband John Wesley Cutrer, a noted criminal lawyer who died on June 10, 1932, the tenth anniversary of the death of their eldest son who drowned in Moon Lake. The Cutrer Mansion, a landmarked building, had been threatened with demolition; and as recently as June 10, 1999, Penny Mayfield, Feature Editor for the Clarksdale *Press Register*, had written an article headlined, "Mansion Demolition Set for July." However, at this writing it looks as though public interest has rallied to save the Cutrer mansion, for the demolition has been postponed with the expectation of funds coming from a number of quarters, both private and public.

Page 84 – MRS. ADAMS: Have you heard what Tom Newby told his mother this morning about what he saw at Moon Lake?

The last name Newby may have been taken from a fellow classmate in the Iowa Theater Department, Hayes A. Newby—later a Professor of Speech—who, in a recent phone interview, still remembers being paired off with Tom Williams by Professor E.C. Mabie to write a Living Newspaper on socialized medicine.

Page 84 – MRS. ADAMS: Heavenly and the Miles boy were seen coming out of a tourist cabin—

Moon Lake is about fifteen miles northeast of Clarksdale, and the Moon Lake Casino still stands—but is a bed and breakfast now called Uncle Henry's. I had dinner there as a participant in the Clarksdale Tennessee Williams Festival of 1998, and coming out the door onto the front porch, looking to the right I can testify that the tourist cabins, too, still stand. Moon Lake Casino is mentioned in a number of TW plays, most memorably in *A Streetcar Named Desire*.

Page 85 – MRS. LAMPHREY: If it does rain, we'll simply move the pahty indoors.

The word "rain" has been added to the sentence for clarity.

Page 86 – MRS. BUFORD: Such peculiar weather! Torrential rains and days like midsummer! I wonder if the levee's in danger?

Throughout SS, the threat of a flood looms as an ominous possibility. Destructive floods visited the Delta in 1882 and 1927, causing loss of life, displacement, and total disruption. The flood of 1882 was probably responsible for Mark Twain revisiting the great river as he was struggling to complete his book *Life on the Mississippi*, published in 1883. And he wrote therein: "The present flood of 1882 will doubtless be celebrated in the river's history for several generations. . . . In some regions south, when the flood was at its highest, the Mississippi was *seventy miles wide*!" (Italics his.)

Page 92 – HENRY: Is that what *they* did to that—you know—that girl across the Sunflower River? (Italics added.)

In AITCM, this speech read "the Klan" instead of "they."

Page 93 – ARTHUR: You've got the instinct for self-destruction.

HEAVENLY: I probably got it from Colonel Wayne. You know he led the charge up Cemetery Hill.

The presumption is that Colonel Wayne died in the charge up Cemetery Hill, but that is never specifically stated in the play. In contrast, the historical record is detailed and complex—and must be noted albeit briefly. According to Shelby Foote, General Lee on July 2, 1863, ordered a main attack on Union forces, and the heights of Cemetery Hill were included in that major assault. Colonel Isaac Avery and Brigadier General Harry T. Hayes led two brigades straight up the steep hill and neither brigade would be stopped. Avery fell at the outset, mortally wounded.

Shortly thereafter, the two heroic brigades were forced to retreat in the face of a Union counterattack. It is Avery, most likely, who is the model for Colonel Wayne—assuming TW was familiar with the historical record. But SS never supplies the details of Colonel Wayne's fate after he charged "right in the face of their guns."

Page 100 – DICK: I been to Friar's Point—

Friar's Point is a dozen or so miles north of Clarksdale and was formerly its rival sister city. Though now diminished into a village, it still sits on the shore of the Mississippi River.

Page 100 – DICK: Heavenly, I've got a job on the government levee project.

Dick has probably been hired by the Army Corps of Engineers as a civilian for a limited time during the current emergency brought on by the spring rain. An article in the New York *Times* (December 8, 1998), "Battle Beside the Levee: Hold Back the Big Muddy or Let It Roll," by Jim Yardley ("A Special Section: The Natural World: WATER," G7), described how the destruction wrought by the 1927 flood caused Congress to assume responsibility for floods, giving the U.S. Army's Corps of Engineers primary responsibility.

Page 101 – DICK: I'm sick of bath salts and spirits of ammonia.

Bath salts are used to soften and scent bathwater; while spirits of ammonia were a common way to revive women who fainted—in a bygone age where women fainted more frequently.

Page 102 – DICK: Ole Mammies with *breakbone fever* ain't good at roof climbing. (Italics added.)

On October 7, 1999, Cable Network News (CNN) reported an outbreak of "breakbone fever" in south Texas, which was described as a viral disease spread by mosquitoes, causing flu-like symptoms of pain behind the eyes and in joints and muscles, accompanied by a rash and fever. Recovery generally takes five to seven days.

Page 103 – DICK: But you can forget Moon Lake last night, or yesterday up on the hill?

"Up on the hill" suggests the opening scene church picnic. But that is impossible for two reasons: the stipulated time is "yesterday," which would be Friday. The church picnic took place—at the latest—the day before on Thursday. But this opening scene picnic cannot be tagged for time with any certainty—though it clearly takes place during the week that precedes the Lamphrey lawn party. Most likely, the picnic took place when church picnics usually take place: on Sunday afternoon. Furthermore, there was little physical affection during the angry exchanges between Heavenly and Dick—certainly nothing memorable. Since "last night at Moon Lake" clearly refers to a sexual encounter, the second phrase would seem to refer to the same kind of romantic intensity, which also happened Friday, making it a very busy day for Heavenly. This may well be another instance where TW has lost sight of the sequential action of a particular version. Lacking a more reasonable alternative, "yesterday" is retained.

Page 103 – HEAVENLY: . . . —a front porch girl!

This speech beginning with "She sits on the front porch..." is an insertion, not a part of TW's final draft of SS. It was found among the discarded out-takes and put in for two reasons: it emphasizes again the major theme of the play at a poignant moment where Heavenly—in the text—recalls Agnes Peabody as the quintessential "front porch girl"; but beyond that, it is an eloquent and moving description of the pathos of a woman waiting.

Page 108-110 – Stage directions: *The scene is the public library.*

This scene, beginning as it does before the rainstorm, seems to be taking place simultaneously with the preceding scene. This requires no great adjustment on the part of the audience and has been left as written.

Page 109 – HERTHA: What lips my lips have kissed. . . .

TW's text does not stipulate the poem, but simply indicates that Hertha reads the poem aloud. This sonnet by Edna St. Vincent Millay from *The Harp Weaver*, (Harper and Brothers, 1923) was picked for two reasons: Millay was one of TW's favorite poets; and the line, "Thus in the winter stands the lonely tree," seemed like it was written for Hertha, who images herself—in truth, becomes—a tree at the end of the first scene.

Page 111 – MISS SCHLAGMANN: How would you like to go to the movies with me next Saturday night, Hertha?

The text reads "tomorrow night"—and a few lines down, Birdie Schlagmann talks about "the Tarzan serial on Saturday night." Once again, TW has lost track of time. For this library scene takes place on the Saturday night of the Lamphrey's lawn party and tomorrow is therefore Sunday, a day when serials were not generally shown. So at the risk of making Ms. Schlagmann a bit less compassionate inviting Hertha to the movies a week hence rather than tomorrow, "next Saturday" has replaced "tomorrow," so that they can see the serial.

Page 111 – HERTHA: I liked that last one of Greta Garbo's.

Greta Garbo made two films where she played doomed women immediate to this period: *Anna Karenina* (1935) and *Camille* (1937).

Page 114 – HERTHA: Lots of them get *dementia praecox* at about that age. . . .

A Latin phrase for schizophrenia. But more important, it is the diagnostic term used to describe TW's sister, Rose, when she was admitted to Farmington State Hospital on July 31, 1937. Hertha then, at least on one level, is TW's attempt to deal with his sister's insanity, since SS was written during and after her early confinement, first at Barnes Hospital in December of 1936 and then at St. Vincent's and Farmington during 1937.

Page 115 – HERTHA: Ask Him that the next time you go to St. George's.

St. George is the name of the Episcopal church in Clarksdale where TW's maternal grandfather, the Reverend Walter Edwin Dakin, served as pastor for fourteen years, until his retirement at the age of seventy-three in 1931.

Page 117 – MISS PEABODY: I bought some of that silk print at Gillam's.

According to staff members at Clarksdale Carnegie Library, Gillam's was a menswear store that went out of business a long time ago. TW remembered the name but forgot the specific line of goods.

Page 118 – MISS PEABODY: Did you ever see such a rain? *Forty-eight hours without a let up.* (Italics added.)

Neither this library scene nor the Lamphrey's lawn party scene just before portray non-stop rain. Is this Miss Peabody's hysterical exaggeration—or TW's oversight?

Page 118 – MISS PEABODY: Oh heavens, it's nearly nine! (and a few lines down, the following stage directions:) [*Hertha slowly raises another book and places it on the shelf. As she does so the clock strikes nine in a slow, gentle tone.*]

In TW's typed text of SS, Miss Peabody exclaims: "Oh heavens it's nearly eleven!" And a few lines down the stage directions correspondingly call for the clock to strike eleven. Since this seemed a very late hour for a municipal library to remain open, I wrote an inquiring letter to Joyce Fulton, Secretary of the Clarksdale Carnegie Public Library; and she responded, after having done some extraordinary research in the archives of the library itself, with the following letter dated March 11, 1997:

"At your request . . . I searched the library board minutes of the 1930s. In the September 1938 minutes the statement was made that the then library hours of 8-7 Mon-Sat—and not open on Sunday—which had been in effect for one year, would be changed back to the hours the library had observed for many years; and they were 9-9 Mon-Sat, and 2:30-6 on Sunday. I hope this will assist you." As a result of Ms. Fulton's information, closing time in the SS text was moved back.

Page 122 – ARTHUR: "Go and catch a falling star, /Get with child a mandrake root!"

The first two lines of John Donne's "Song," though the opening line quoted here frequently serves as its title.

Page 126 – HEAVENLY: You don't know how it feels!
    LILA: Yes, I do know! And I know it's hard to be young! Almost as hard as it is to be old!

Aunt Lila's entire speech (and the brief line preceding from Heavenly that sets it up) is not in TW's final SS text, but was found in the outtakes. It has been inserted because of its simple eloquence and wisdom.

Page 127 – AUNT LILA: Here smoke your cigarette. Cigarettes were made for moments like these. Girls didn't smoke 'em back in the days when I had my big romantic catastrophes.

Concerning Heavenly and her pronounced cigarette habit, encouraged by the one adult in her house whom she respects and listens to: one scene among the out-takes depicts Arthur teaching Heavenly to smoke; while another few surviving pages of a discarded scene catches the moment when Dick levels with Heavenly about his feelings for her immediately after they have had sexual intercourse, admitting that he desires her but does not love her. Heavenly's response is to ask for a cigarette. When Dick says he has none, she explodes. "HEAVENLY: I've got to have a cigarette. You *know* I have to have a cigarette" (italics in text). Significantly, TW meant to underline Heavenly's two addictions: nicotine and caffeine—a matter of greater interest and sensitivity today than in the period in which TW wrote.

Page 128 – LILA: When they've got the itch in them shoes there's nothing but six feet of dirt can ever make 'em stay put.

In the TW typed text of SS, this line is Heavenly's, but its style and substance seem more naturally to belong to Lila. Therefore, the speech has been given to Lila, breaking up the exchange between the two characters and allowing Heavenly to respond: "Tell me what to do."

Page 129 – MRS. CRITCHFIELD: Heavenly! Arthur's sent you a corsage! To wear to the Country Club tonight.

For chronological sense, Mrs. Critchfield's lines "To wear to the dinner tonight" and "It's going to look lovely on her white organdy" were changed to "To wear to the Country Club tonight" and "It's going to look lovely on your blue knitted suit," respectively. Additionally, Mrs. Critchfield's line "I've simply worked miracles on that dress" has been cut since it is obvious that the remaking of the dress belongs to the preparations for the lawn party and not for the evening after.

Page 131 – HEAVENLY: Didn't I open your eyes when I told you what had been going on between him and me?

The original SS text read "when I told you *yesterday*"—which is another chronological mistake, so the word was simply deleted. Yesterday was the Lamphrey's lawn party. And it was the day before yesterday that Heavenly told her mother about her sexual relationship with Dick. Various small adjustments have been made in the scene to indicate that the Lamphrey party is in the past, not the future.

Page 134 – MRS. CRITCHFIELD: Oh, my dear boy, it's started raining again!

Again for chronological sense, all of Mrs. Critchfield's lines have suffered a tense change to accord with the fact that the Lamphrey's party took place the night before.

Page 138 – Stage direction: [*Heavenly enters. Her eyes have a hectic brilliance.*]

In the SS manuscript there was an additional stage direction: "*In her white organdy dress with the orchid pinned to her shoulder she is a breathtaking vision,*" which has been cut to avoid confusion about the chronology of the plot.

Page 138 – ARTHUR: I thought you weren't going to the Country Club.

This line was changed from "I thought you weren't going to the Lamphrey's," since the lawn party already took place in a previous scene and the Country Club dinner is scheduled for the current scene.

Page 148 – HEAVENLY: I'm going out and sit on the front porch till one of them comes back.

This open-ended ending, far superior to the second provocative conclusion to AITCM—see the Introduction, pp. xv and xvi— is truly a defeat for the high-spirited Heavenly who places herself into the solitary confinement of a Front Porch Girl, a woman without a beau to take her places. Heavenly has fallen into the hell of a life without options. But after World War II, after the Freedom Riders and the sexual revolution of the 60s, after the Civil Rights Bill signed by President Lyndon Johnson, this kind of settled southern small town life would be as gone with the wind as the antebellum South it still remembered and grieved for—even as its young men rejected it by moving to the North and the East, leaving behind a legacy of Front Porch Girls. But at least *Spring Storm* has survived, written by Tom Williams with love and sadness, reason enough for celebration.

—Dan Isaac